VAMPIRE BRAT

·4·
ARAMINTA SPOOK

VAMPIRE BRAT

as told to
ANGIE SAGE

illustrated by
JIMMY PICKERING

BLOOMSBURY

First published in Great Britain in 2007 by Bloomsbury Publishing Plc
36 Soho Square, London, W1D 3QY

Published in America by HarperCollins Children's Books,
a division of HarperCollins Publishers, 1350 Avenue of the Americas,
New York NY 10019

A CIP catalogue record of this book is available from the British Library

ISBN 978 0 7475 8349 3

All papers used by Bloomsbury Publishing are natural, recyclable products made from
wood grown in well-managed forests. The manufacturing processes conform to the
environmental regulations of the country of origin.

Printed in Italy by L.E.G.O. S.p.A

1 3 5 7 9 10 8 6 4 2

www.aramintaspook.co.uk

For James, Amelia,
and Katharine, with love

CONTENTS

VAMPIRE BRAT

~1~

BAT POO

Things have been happening in Spook House—weird werewolf and vampire things.

It all started when Aunt Tabby tripped over Sir Horace's treasure chest. Sir Horace is our best ghost. He lives inside a suit of armour and wanders around Spook House, so you never know where he is going to turn up next. Recently I rescued his ancient treasure

chest from his old castle, and since then it has been sitting in the hall because it is so heavy that no one wants to move it. I liked it being in the hall but Aunt Tabby did not. She said it smelled funny, which is true, but then so do a lot of things in Spook House.

You probably know that Brenda, Barry, and Wanda Wizzard all live in Spook House with me and my Aunt Tabby and Uncle Drac, which can be quite fun. It can also be very annoying. And this day was one of the annoying ones.

"That chest will have to go," said Aunt Tabby, rubbing her shin. "Go and get Barry to help you take it upstairs out of the way."

Barry, who is Wanda's dad, did not want to take the chest upstairs out of the way. He said he had enough smelly, heavy weights to lift as it was. But Aunt Tabby won as usual, and Wanda and I helped Barry take the chest up to the ghost-in-the-bath bathroom at the top of the stairs. There is definitely no ghost-in-the-bath there any more, which I know because I have waited there for hours trying to catch a ghost having a bath with no luck at all. Anyway, why would a ghost *want* to have a bath? They don't need to, since they do not get dirty.

We had just dumped the treasure chest down beside the bath when Brenda, who is Wanda's mum, came in. Her cat, Pusskins, had been missing for three days, and Brenda was getting slightly hysterical.

"Is Pusskins in there?" she asked, pointing at the treasure chest.

"I don't think so," said Wanda. "Pusskins wouldn't like the smell."

I did not think that was true because Pusskins is a smelly cat. "Maybe Pusskins *is* the smell," I suggested.

Brenda gave a little scream. "Open it, open it," she yelled. So we did. Pusskins was not there. Barry took Brenda away to sit down somewhere quiet.

Sir Horace had already shown us what was in the treasure chest, but since it was open, Wanda and I took another look, just in case he had missed something interesting the first time. But he hadn't. There was no real treasure at all, just lots of papers, Sir Horace's mouldy lucky rabbit's foot, and a battered old silver whistle. In fact Sir Horace had already given us the only treasure—two gold medals—which we always kept under our pillows.

Brenda spent the rest of the morning walking around Spook House going, "Here pussy-kins, come here, my little puss-cat, come to your mummy-wummy . . ." and general yucky stuff like that. Even Wanda, who can be a bit like that herself, got tired of it. But Brenda would not stop. I think she loves Pusskins more than anything else in the world—

although I suppose she might prefer Wanda a *little* bit more, but it would be a close call. Pusskins is not even a particularly nice cat; she likes to hiss at you if she thinks you are doing anything wrong. She is also quite fat and getting fatter all the time, because whatever Wanda may say, I *know* she feeds Pusskins my cheese and onion crisps.

By the afternoon even Aunt Tabby was getting tired of Brenda moping around looking for Pusskins, so she said we had to help search the house. She and Brenda were going to start at the top, and Wanda and I had to start in the basement. Then we would all meet in the middle.

I like the basement of Spook House. It is full of wiggly, winding corridors that lead to little kitchens, big kitchens, laundry rooms, larders, junk rooms, and all kinds of hidden places. A secret passage runs behind some of the walls, too. I have been down there a few times, but to get to it you have to go through a little door underneath the attic stairs right at the top of the house. Then you have to go down in a scary lift thingy and a rickety ladder. I have often thought there must be a quicker way to get there—like a secret door somewhere in the basement too, but I have never found it.

Although I did not tell Wanda, I decided not to waste my time looking for Pusskins, who would not come to me however nicely I called her. I do not like Pusskins and Pusskins does not like me. As Uncle Drac says, the feeling is mutual. So while Wanda went off down the big corridor that goes past all the kitchens, calling out, "Pusskins, here pussy-kins," and sounding just like a squeaky version of Brenda, I zoomed off down the corridor that leads to the bat poo hatch. I was heading for Creepy Corner, where Barry keeps all the sacks to put the poo in, as I have never had time to explore there. Somehow Aunt Tabby always knows where I am and says, "I really don't know why you want to go down *there*, Araminta. Come away at once." But this time I knew Aunt Tabby was far away, at the very top of Spook House. In fact she and Brenda were out on the roof, looking for Pusskins. I was safe. Well, safe from Aunt Tabby anyway.

The bat poo hatch is at the bottom of Uncle Drac's turret, where he keeps all his bats. Every day Wanda's dad, Barry, shovels the bat poo into sacks, which is why, as I turned the corner, my way was blocked by a huge pile of bat poo, and a voice said, "What are *you* doing here, Araminta?"

"I am looking for Pusskins," I told him, even though that was not entirely true, as I was really looking for a secret door. But it wasn't really a fib because obviously if I found Pusskins I would not ignore her.

Barry's face appeared just above the poo. He looked suspicious. "Have you hidden Pusskins, too?" he asked.

I sighed. I knew this was because of the frogs. Barry has some acrobatic frogs and they can do some good tricks. You would think that would make him a fun kind of person but it does not. He is generally grumpy and suspicious.

For instance, he thinks I stole his frogs not

long ago, which I did not. In fact *I* tracked them down and returned them to him.

Was he pleased? No.

Did he say, "Oh thank you so much, Araminta, I am eternally grateful"? No, he did not.

So I shall not bother with the frogs again. They are more trouble that you could possibly believe. Still, Aunt Tabby says I should make an effort to be polite, so I said, "And how are your frogs, Barry? Are they well?"

He gave a funny smile and said, "You're not fooling me that easily, Araminta." Then he continued shovelling bat poo.

"Excuse me," I said in my best Aunt Tabby voice. "Please may I get past?"

"No, you may not," Barry replied. "I have just spent the last hour shovelling bat poo and I am not going to spend another hour shovelling it all back in just so that you can wander by. In fact I've got another shovel here if you want to help fill up these sacks."

"No thank you, Barry," I said.

Now, if you don't know about Spook House, then you probably wonder why Barry was shovelling bat poo. My Uncle Drac keeps tons of bats in his bat turret. He used to run a bat poo business but now he knits instead. For a long time the bat poo just piled up and got totally disgusting until Barry took over the bat poo business. Now Barry shovels it out through the poo hatch in the basement (although Uncle Drac still does some at night), then he puts it into sacks and sells it at the garden gate. He gives Uncle Drac half the money, which Uncle Drac uses to buy lots of weird yarn for his new knitting business. I think he is knitting gherkins at the moment. He gave me a knitted bar of chocolate for my birthday, which was OK I suppose, but I would rather have had a real one.

Barry disappeared through the bat poo hatch to get another shovel load. As soon as he had left, I held my nose tight and climbed over the pile of bat poo. It was disgusting—all squishy and my shoes sank right into it. Why would people want to buy that stuff?

I had never been past the bat poo hatch before and I was really excited—and not a bit scared. Not really. I was sure that any minute now I would find a secret door just like the one under the attic stairs that would open straight into the secret passage that winds inside the basement walls.

As soon as I got around Creepy Corner, the

corridor got really dark, so I switched on my torch, which I always have in my pocket. I was surprised how narrow it was. And it was full of empty sacks, all piled up waiting for bat poo. I squeezed past them and set off down the narrow winding passage. I could tell that no one had been there for years, as the spiders' webs were huge. They felt like sticky bits of string and got tangled in my hair. Great big spiders were dropping off them all over the place. I was glad that Wanda was not with me because she hates spiders and when one lands on her she yells so loud that my ears feel funny.

But when I went around the next corner I really wished that Wanda *was* with me. Because suddenly I heard a low, rumbling growl from somewhere nearby. I was so scared that I dropped my torch, and as it fell the beam of light lit up two glittery eyes. I didn't dare move. Another long growl made my hair stand up on end and two green eyes glinted at me out of the dark. That was *not* Pusskins. Pusskins may make some weird noises but I have never heard her *growl*, and besides, her eyes would not be three feet off the ground like these were. Whatever it was was a whole lot bigger than Pusskins, that was for sure.

It felt like forever as the eyes stared at me and I stared back. But I did not do my fiendish stare or anything like that. I stared at them because I didn't dare look away. And I didn't dare look away because I had worked out what they were—they were *werewolf* eyes—and if you look away from werewolf eyes for even a split second, the werewolf will pounce. Your only hope is to walk backwards very slowly and then run for it.

And that is what I did. I left my torch where it had fallen and I *ran*. Straight into the pile of bat poo. Yuck.

THUNDER

Wanda did not believe that I had seen a werewolf.

I found her in the boiler room eating a whole bag of gummi bears and warming her hands on the boiler. She was not looking very hard for Pusskins if you ask me. Anyway, I rushed in, covered in bat poo, and Wanda did not look at all pleased to see me.

"Ugh," she said, jumping away. "Don't get

that stuff all over me. Or the boiler. Mum will be really annoyed."

Wanda's mother, Brenda, takes care of the boiler. She does it extremely well and the boiler room is very nice now. The boiler is polished, the floor is swept, and there is a little line of coal buckets and an alarm clock. Every three hours the alarm clock rings and either Barry or Brenda feeds the boiler with a bucket of coal. Sometimes even Uncle Drac does it, but Aunt Tabby does not, which I think is a good thing because Aunt Tabby and boilers do not mix. But that day the boiler room was not so great, as Brenda had been looking for Pusskins, and the boiler was making funny gurgling noises—or maybe it was Wanda.

I made Wanda give me some gummi bears

and told her all about the growling and the werewolf eyes. But she did not believe me.

"But, Araminta," she said in the voice she uses for telling me something that she thinks I don't know. "Everyone knows that were-wolves are just normal people during the day, so it can't be a werewolf. And if there *is* a werewolf in Spook House it is going to be someone who lives here. Like your Aunt Tabitha—or *you*. In fact," she said, looking at

me in a funny way, "all things considered, it probably *is* you."

It is tough always having to explain things to Wanda but I've got used to it. "Look, Wanda," I said very patiently, "obviously it is not me. I would *know* if I was a werewolf, wouldn't I? And actually, if I *was* a werewolf I do not think *you* would still be around. I think I would have eaten you for supper before now."

Wanda did not answer. She stuffed another handful of gummi bears in her mouth and didn't offer me *any*. So I continued telling her about the werewolf. "It was *horrible*. You would have been really scared. It growled and it had big yellow fangs and lots of matted fur. And claws. And it drooled. *Tons* of drool. All over the floor." Although I hadn't actually *seen* all that stuff, that is what the pictures in my *Werewolf Spotter's Handbook* showed, so it must have looked like that.

Wanda began to look a bit scared. "Really?" she asked, gulping down the last gummi bear.

I nodded.

"Supposing he creeps up on us here," she whispered, glancing around.

I hadn't really thought of that. I had reckoned that Barry and his pile of bat poo would be enough to keep any werewolf at bay, but I was beginning to think it would be nice to get out of the basement just in case. And then something really spooky happened. There was a great big bang and all the lights flickered off and on, off and on. Wanda screamed and we both *ran*.

We bumped into Brenda, who was coming down the basement stairs.

"Wanda, Araminta," she said, "there's the most awful thunderstorm. Come into the kitchen where it's safe." Brenda grabbed hold of us both and took us into the third-kitchen-on-the-right-just-around-the-corner-past-the-boiler-room. Before we knew it we were sitting at the table eating Brenda's egg and lettuce sandwiches—except the lettuce in mine had mysteriously managed to escape and fall on the floor. Lettuce in Spook House always tastes of bat poo, because that is what Aunt Tabby feeds her lettuces with. Yuck. And now that Brenda keeps a load of weird chickens in the back garden, all the sandwiches she makes have egg in them. Egg and banana, egg and jelly, egg and peanut butter, egg and frog— well, not yet, but it is only a matter of time. I only like egg sandwiches if I can have some cheese and onion crisps with them to take the eggy taste away, so I went to get a bag from my crisp cupboard *but they were all gone.*

"Whararyoudoing?" said Wanda, spraying bits of egg all over the table.

"Don't spray egg all over the table, dear," said Brenda.

"I am looking for my crisps," I said frostily.

"Oh, they're not there," said Wanda, who often likes to tell me things that are what Uncle Drac calls totally obvious.

"You have been feeding them to Pusskins again, haven't you?" I said.

"Wanda, do you know where Pusskins is?" asked Brenda, looking a bit suspicious. She was getting as bad as Barry.

"No, I *don't*," said Wanda. "Araminta is fibbing as usual."

"I am not."

"Yes, you are."

"No, I am *not*."

"Girls, girls," said Brenda, "*do* stop fighting. Oh my *goodness*!"

A huge crash of thunder shook the house, all the lights went off, and a ghostly phone bell started to ring . . . and ring . . . and ring.

Brenda and Wanda dived under the table, but I do not dive under tables.

"I am going upstairs," I told them, "to watch the lightning."

Halfway up the big stairs from the hall I met Sir Horace. He was on the landing. Sir Horace is my most favourite ghost ever. We do have another one, but he is not much fun in my opinion, although Wanda likes him. His name is Edmund and he lives in the secret passage behind the boiler. But Sir Horace is wonderful. He lives in an old suit of armour and he just hangs around the house. He is not good at climbing stairs and he forgets that it takes him days to get all the way up— although sometimes, by mistake, he goes down really fast.

I stopped beside Sir Horace, tapped very quietly on his armour, and said, "Are you awake?" Sir Horace spends a lot of time dozing and it is a good idea not to surprise him when he is asleep. He often wakes up with a jump and then parts of his armour fall off. You do not want parts of Sir Horace to fall off halfway up the stairs. Last week, when he was only two steps from the top, the spring holding his left knee together pinged out, his leg dropped off, and he fell all the way down to

the bottom. It was not my fault at all, I just happened to be walking past at the time, but no one believed me. I spent the rest of the day putting Sir Horace back together again.

"**Good morning, Miss Spook.**" Sir Horace's booming voice came out from his helmet.

"It's not morning any more, Sir Horace. It's nearly dinner time now," I said.

"**Is it really? How time flies when you're going upstairs.**"

"Sir Horace," I said, very quickly, as Sir Horace does go on a bit and it is best to get your question in early. "Have you seen a were-wolf around here?"

There was another crash of thunder and the lights came back on, flickered, and then went off again.

"**A what wolf?**" asked Sir Horace.

"A *were*wolf."

"Where? Ah, indeed, that is the question, Miss Spook. Where does one find wolves nowadays? In my time we used to have them howling at the castle gates on a cold winter's night. Terrible noise it was. Quite froze the blood . . ."

"Wow. Did it really, Sir Horace?"

"Yes, it most certainly did, Miss Spook. Ah, those were the days. You know I once found an abandoned wolf cub?"

"Did you really?" Now that was interesting.

"Indeed I did, Miss Spook. It had injured its leg and been deserted by the wolf pack. I took it home and raised it myself. A wonderful companion. . . ." Sir Horace sighed like he always does when he remembers the old days, which in his case are extremely old days. "Ah well," he said, "I must be getting along." He suddenly stuck one foot out and put it on the next step. He looked very wobbly.

"Would you like some help, Sir Horace?" I asked.

"That would be most welcome, Miss Spook," said Sir Horace in a smiley kind of voice. So I took his right arm—very carefully—and we got to the top of the stairs in no time at all. **"Along here, if you please, Miss Spook,"** said Sir Horace, so I walked along with him to the little secret door under the attic stairs.

Now I knew where Sir Horace was heading—he was going to his secret room. I helped him open the door and watched as he squeezed through, then I closed the door behind him. I listened to his footsteps fading away down the secret passage that runs behind the wooden panelling on the wall, and then a loud crash of thunder reminded me that I had an urgent appointment with some lightning.

I ran down the corridor, through two mouldy curtains, and past the monster bathroom. I zoomed along the zigzag passage, jumped over the trapdoor to nowhere, climbed up the old apple ladder and scrambled on to the ledge. And there I was, outside the old door to the haunted turret. I turned the key and went inside.

~3~
LIGHTNING

There are lots of turrets in Spook House, but the best one to watch thunderstorms from is the haunted turret. The haunted turret is not really haunted. Well, *I've* never seen a ghost there and I have spent many hours looking. But it is the tallest turret and is so high in the sky that you feel as though you are right in the middle of the storm. It is very exciting.

After you push open the little door with
the weird creak that goes "Eeh-aaaah . . .
ooooh," you climb up some rickety, cobwebby
stairs, but you must not step on the third stair
or the seventh because they are rotten because
of some very big woodworms who live there.
The stairs go round two corners and are really
dark and steep. At the top is a dusty old velvet
curtain, which is inhabited by some fierce
moths that do not like being disturbed and
dive-bomb your head, so it is best to squeeze
through the curtain very slowly and carefully.
Once you are in the turret you have to walk
around the edge because there is a big hole in
the middle of the floor where a bathtub fell
through. Aunt Tabby used to keep lots of old
bathtubs in the turret, but she made Barry
help her take them all out after that.

Anyway, as I carefully walked around the edge of the turret I was really happy to see a bright flash of lightning. I stopped and counted the seconds until the loud crash of thunder came. It was not even two seconds, more like one and a half. That meant that the middle of the storm—the exciting part where the lightning is right overhead—was really close. Great, I thought, I'm here just in time. I climbed on to an old box by the window so that I could see out, as the window is very high up. It is also very dirty, as Aunt Tabby does not clean windows because it lets the light in and Aunt Tabby thinks that houses should be nice and gloomy, which is why she paints everything brown. I think she would even paint *me* brown if I stood still for long enough.

I rubbed a clean patch on the glass and
peered out. Even though it was
not yet dinner time it
was almost dark out-
side. There were

heavy grey clouds filling up the sky and a few fat spots of rain were falling. It was perfect— and really spooky.

In the distance, all misty through the rain and the grubby window, I saw a car's head-lights. I watched the lights, expecting them to keep going along the big road, but to my surprise the car turned off into the lane that goes by Spook House. I wondered where it was going—since Aunt Tabby put up a sign that says DANGER, UNEXPLODED MINES not many cars drive past. As it drew nearer I could see that it was going really slowly, as if it was looking for somewhere, and then it stopped—right outside our front gate.

At the very moment that it drew up outside Spook House there was the most enormous *Craaaack*. A brilliant white streak of lightning shot down and hit the car. It was amazing. A blue flame whizzed around the outside of the car and I held my breath, waiting for it to explode.

It was very disappointing—nothing happened. The car did not explode at all. Instead the rain started to pour from the sky in buckets and the car didn't even *sizzle*. It was a weird car. It was very long and I knew I had seen cars like that before but I could not think where. The window was misting up with my breath, so I rubbed it again and then I could see more clearly. The car outside Spook House was a hearse! *With a coffin in it.*

I wished I had Wanda's telescope. I could just about see three people sitting in the back of the hearse with the coffin—a girl who looked almost grown-up, a little kid, and an old lady. The driver was sitting on his own in the front; he wore a top hat and had a very white face that almost shone through the window.

All the time I was watching the hearse, thunder was rolling around the sky, and in the distance every now and then lightning streaked down from the clouds. The rain was falling harder now, it was splashing in through the rotten window frame and dripping on to my socks. I rubbed the window clear with the end of my sleeve, and when I looked again the white-faced driver had got out. He opened an enormous black umbrella, and was holding the door open for the old lady. She stepped out of the hearse very carefully and was followed by the little kid and the almost grown-up girl.

Even though I did not want to be a detective any more because now I had decided that I was going to be a werewolf hunter, I still practised my detecting skills when I got the chance. I thought the people in the hearse were on their way to a funeral. That was pretty obvious because if they had been on their way back from the funeral, the coffin would not have been there. And it was obvious that they were going to a funeral and not just taking the coffin out for a ride in a thunderstorm because they were dressed in black and were wearing hats. The old lady had a veil covering her face and the little kid had a funny black cap on. I watched the almost grown-up girl get out of the hearse. She wore a really great black hat perched on the back of her head and a black dress almost down to the ground, the kind that I would not mind wearing when I grow up. She lifted the hem of the dress out of the way of the huge puddle that always lurks outside our gate when it rains and she tiptoed up the path underneath the umbrella along with the old lady, while the little kid hung back in the rain and looked like he didn't want to be here.

A flash of lightning lit up the purple sky, and there was a sudden crash as the thunder rolled back over the house. Far away downstairs, I heard the doorbell ring.

Yes! We had a hearse with a coffin and spooky visitors in the middle of a thunderstorm. What could be better?

~4~
THE HEARSE PARTY

I made it down to the front door at the same time as Aunt Tabby—in fact I bumped into her as she was climbing back inside through the dome thingy that leads on to the roof. She was dripping wet and not in a good mood. We raced all the way down to the hall and it was a dead heat, although as Aunt Tabby has longer arms than me she reached the door handle first. There was no

sign of Brenda, who usually races Aunt Tabby to the door, so I guessed she was still hiding under the kitchen table with wimpy Wanda.

Aunt Tabby threw open the huge old front door to Spook House and went sort of pale. Her mouth opened but she did not say anything, which was very unlike Aunt Tabby, who always has something to say even when you wish she hadn't.

All four of the strangers just stood out there in the rain staring at Aunt Tabby and me. They did not smile or say anything. They had deathly white faces and narrow eyes that bored right through you and out to the other side. I felt like one of those turret steps that the woodworm had eaten. It was weird.

Aunt Tabby made a kind of cough/croak noise, which could have meant almost anything

at all. None of the hearse party replied. A strange yellow light came from the distant lightning flashes and all the time the rain pelted down. It ran down the silent people's faces and dripped off the ends of their noses.

Suddenly Aunt Tabby woke up. She shook herself and yelled in a kind of panicky voice, "Drac! Drac! Your mother's here!"

Wow! I had no idea that Uncle Drac had a *mother*.

I did not think that Aunt Tabby was being very polite, as she always says you should not yell for someone, you should go and find them and ask them *nicely*, Araminta. And also she had not even asked the visitors in, and one of them was her mother-in-law, which meant that she was my great-aunt, so I decided to be polite and show Aunt Tabby what you should do.

"Good afternoon, Great-aunt," I said, since I did not know her name. "Welcome to Spook House. Please come in." Then I stepped back right on to Aunt Tabby's toes and Aunt Tabby yelped. But I must have said the right thing because the old lady strode into the house. She was scary—but what was even scarier was a double-headed dead ferret that she wore around her neck, which stared at me with its four glass eyes as she swept by. The driver shook the umbrella out, carefully placed it in the monster umbrella stand by the door, and went back to the car.

The little kid, who looked like a drowned rat, trotted in next, and he was followed by the almost grown-up girl. She was wearing black lacy socks and cute little black boots. I smiled at her and she half smiled back—I think. They all stood lined up in the hall and said nothing. The only sound you could hear was water dripping on to the floor.

There was another crash of thunder and the front door suddenly slammed shut. *Bang!* Aunt Tabby and I jumped about three feet in the air.

And then Uncle Drac's mother spoke. "Well, Tabitha," she said in a scratchy kind of voice. "We meet again." She did not exactly sound pleased about it, I thought.

Aunt Tabby gulped like one of Barry's frogs and then she hissed in my ear, "Where *is* Drac? Go and fetch him, Araminta. Quick!"

I didn't really want to go because I thought the creepy relatives were really interesting, but I could see that Aunt Tabby needed help and fast, so I raced up the big stairs and along the landing until I found the little red door to Uncle Drac's turret.

Uncle Drac generally sleeps in the day because he does not like the light very much. On the other side of Spook House from the haunted turret there is a really tall turret—this is where Uncle Drac keeps his bats. Aunt Tabby has been trying to make Uncle Drac get rid of all the bats since Barry does not sell enough bat poo and it keeps piling up inside the turret. But Uncle Drac loves his bats. Last month Aunt Tabby told him that he had to decide between her and the bats, but Uncle Drac took so long trying to make up his mind that Aunt Tabby decided to forget that she had said anything and the bats stayed—and so did she.

I like going to see Uncle Drac in his turret since I am not really allowed there because it is very dangerous. There are no floors to stand on—Uncle Drac took them all out so that the bats can fly around as much as they like and pretend that they are in a really big bat cave.

I carefully pushed open the little red door and peered in. Uncle Drac was fast asleep in his big flowery sleeping bag. You may be wondering where Uncle Drac puts his sleeping bag if there aren't any floors, although you have probably guessed—he hangs it from the rafters.

"Hellooo . . ." I called very quietly, as it is

not a good idea to wake up Uncle Drac very suddenly because he can jump out of his sleeping bag if he gets a shock, which happened once when Big Bat landed on his head. Uncle Drac broke both his legs, but they are OK now. "Hellooo . . ." I called again. "Wake up, Uncle Drac."

Uncle Drac stirred. "WharrisitMinty?" he muttered.

"Your mother's here, Uncle Drac."

"*What?*" Uncle Drac's eyes slammed open

and he nearly leaped right out of his sleeping bag.

"Careful!" I said.

It was OK—just. Uncle Drac kind of slid back down into his sleeping bag and groaned. "Mother . . . *here*?"

"Yes. She's come to see you. Isn't that nice?"

"Nice?" asked Uncle Drac, sounding puzzled. And then he said in a really worried voice, "Oh my goodness, where's Tabby?"

"She's downstairs, Uncle Drac."

"With *Mother*?"

"Yes."

As soon as I said that, Uncle Drac clambered out of his sleeping bag, swung himself up on to the rafter, and walked like a tightrope walker to the door and squeezed through. "Come on, Minty," he said, grabbing hold of my hand, "we can't leave Tabby alone with Mother a moment longer," and we ran down the stairs to the hall.

It was empty. Everyone had disappeared. There was nothing left but a great big steaming puddle of water.

This was getting better and better. Everyone had vaporised!

~5~

MAX DRAC

I t was very disappointing. No one had vaporised at all. Uncle Drac and I found them all sitting at the long table in the third-kitchen-on-the-right-just-around-the-corner-past-the-boiler-room. Brenda and Wanda had managed to crawl out from underneath the table, and Wanda was helping to pour the hot water into Brenda's biggest teapot—which is about the size of a bucket.

The whole kitchen smelled of wet wool—Uncle Drac's mother, the weird little kid, and the almost grown-up girl were sitting at the table, steaming quietly as their thick black clothes began to dry off. No one said a word. Aunt Tabby sat glaring at the end of the table while Uncle Drac's mother was busy eyeballing her in the kind of way that Aunt Tabby sometimes eyeballs me.

Close up I could see that you could not mistake Uncle Drac's mother for anyone else in a million years. She looked just like him. She had the same square, pale face and the same brilliant pointy teeth that just showed over the corners of her mouth—but she did not smile like Uncle Drac. She glowered. So did the double-headed ferret.

The almost grown-up girl looked very

interesting. She had long dark hair with black ribbons threaded through it, and I really liked her little black hat, which had lots of black lace and feathers all over it. I thought I saw a stuffed mouse on it too, but I was not sure and I didn't want to stare too hard. The almost grown-up girl looked like she might not appreciate that.

The little kid was weird. He had squinty eyes and a really pale face like he had never, ever been out in the sun. His shiny black hair was swept back and you could still see the comb marks in it. He was wearing a starched white collar, a tie, and a buttoned-up jacket, and he was sitting on *my* chair, with his little legs swinging to and fro. He was quite podgy and was busy chewing a sweet. I could see he had a great big bag of sweets stuffed into each pocket but he wasn't about to offer any to Wanda or me.

I gave him my fiendish frog stare but he stared right back and he didn't blink. Not once. That had never happened to me before.

Suddenly Uncle Drac broke the silence. "Hello, Mother," he said. "You remember Araminta." Then he said to me, "Minty, this is your Great-aunt Emilene."

I smiled and was about to say hello when Great-aunt Emilene snorted like a camel and said,

"I remember Araminta. Odd little thing."

Well. *She* got a fiendish frog stare too, and the almost grown-up girl almost smiled.

"And these, Minty, are your cousins, Mathilda and Maximilian," said Uncle Drac.

I had heard Uncle Drac talking about them sometimes but I had never met them before. "Hello," I said. Mathilda just smiled kind of mysteriously and Maximilian shoved another sweet in his mouth and kept on chewing. I was really glad that the almost grown-up girl was my cousin, but I could have done without the little kid.

Great-aunt Emilene did her camel impression again and said in a loud voice, "Well, Drac, you're looking peaky. I see Tabitha is still not feeding you properly."

"Oh . . . er . . ." Uncle Drac did not seem

to know what to say, and Aunt Tabby said nothing at all, which really surprised me.

"I did not receive a reply to my letter, Drac," said his mother sternly.

Uncle Drac blinked. "What letter?" he asked.

"Don't make excuses, Drac. As I was saying, I did not get a reply to my letter so I came anyway. Maximilian's parents have been called away on an urgent assignment. I expect you know how successful their ghost-hunting business is now. A good deal more successful than the *bat* poo business, I would imagine."

She sniffed loudly and I thought Uncle Drac looked upset. But she didn't care, she just carried on in her scratchy voice, like chalk squeaking on a blackboard, "Well, Drac, as I said in my letter, Mathilda is off to college and I have a cruise booked that I have *no* intention of missing. Maximilian's trunk is in the car. You can help Perkins out with it and then we'll be gone."

At the mention of "gone", I saw Aunt Tabby smile faintly, but Uncle Drac looked like something had hit him over the head. "Trunk?" he asked.

His mother sighed just like Aunt Tabby sighs when I say something that she does not agree with. "Help Perkins lift it out, will you, Drac?"

Just then Brenda put the teapot down on the table with such a thump that everyone and everything, including all the cups, jumped. "Oops, sorry. Clumsy me," Brenda trilled rather nervously. She started pouring the tea, and I went and sat down at the end of the table. Wanda came and sat next to me, then she leaned over and said right in my ear, "It will be nice to have Maximilian staying with us, won't it, Araminta? I told him he could have our Saturday bedroom."

"What?" I gasped. The Saturday bedroom is my favourite bedroom.

"It will be such fun," said Wanda, who had obviously not noticed that I most definitely did not think it would be anything *like* fun. "We can sleep in our Friday bedroom on Saturday, too. That would be really exciting."

Wanda's idea of what is exciting is not exactly the same as mine.

I looked at Aunt Tabby—surely she was going to say something about this? But she didn't say a thing. She just sat there like a goldfish whose water has just been poured down the sink.

"Um . . . trunk. I'd, er, better go and get it then," muttered Uncle Drac. He gulped down his tea and stood up. His chair made a horrible scraping sound on the floor, but I didn't mind because even that was better than listening to the weird slurping noise that Great-aunt Emilene made while she sucked up her tea like a vacuum cleaner.

There was no way I was going to stay down in that kitchen with Wanda Wizzard grinning at the little kid like he was her new best friend, so I said, "I'll help you, Uncle Drac."

"Would you, Minty?" Uncle Drac looked pleased. He grabbed my hand and we both shot out of the kitchen like we were being chased by a whole pack of werewolves. In fact give me a pack of werewolves any day.

It was pouring with rain when we got outside and the thunder was still rumbling, which was fun. Perkins was asleep in the driver's seat. His mouth was wide open and he was snoring loudly. Uncle Drac tapped on his window, but there was no chance Perkins would hear anything with a snore almost as loud as the thunder.

"You'll have to bang on the window really hard," I told Uncle Drac, who is quite shy and usually leaves all the loud stuff to Aunt Tabby. He didn't seem to want to, so I thumped the window hard and made my cross-eyed wide-mouth frog face through the steamed-up glass.

It worked. Perkins jumped up like something had bitten him, squashed his top hat on the roof of the car, and sat straight back down again. Then he wound down the window and said, "Yeeeees?" in a low, spooky kind of voice that would have really scared Wanda, though it did not scare me at all.

Uncle Drac coughed and said, "We have come for Maximilian's trunk."

Perkins—who looked like a skeleton close up—pushed open the door and nearly knocked us over. A moment later he had opened the back of the hearse and was tugging at the coffin. "A little assistance would not be amiss," he said in his eerie voice.

Uncle Drac and I looked at each other.

Who was in the coffin? And why were they going to be buried in Spook House?

"Not the . . . coffin," said Uncle Drac. "Maximilian's trunk."

Perkins looked at Uncle Drac like he was being really stupid. "This *is* Maximilian's trunk," he said.

Uncle Drac and I heaved the coffin up the crumbling steps to Spook House while Perkins the skeleton watched us through his steamy window, safely back in his nice dry car. We staggered through the front door and dumped the coffin down in the hall with a huge *thump*, which shook the house and brought Aunt Tabby running.

"What is *that*?" she asked, staring at the coffin.

"Trunk," gasped Uncle Drac, sitting down on it and wiping the water out of his eyes. "Minty and I carried it in."

I had never seen Aunt Tabby make a startled horse expression before, so I was very interested in what she was going to say next, but she just whinnied like you had run out of sugar lumps and rolled her eyes.

Then Wanda appeared. *She was holding Maximilian's hand.*

He was trotting beside her, his short little

legs, which were even shorter than Wanda's—
if that is possible—having trouble keeping up
as Wanda dragged him across the hall and
started up the big cobwebby stairs that sweep
up from the hall. "Come on, Max," said
Wanda, sounding like she was trying to get
one of Barry's frogs to do a particularly diffi-
cult jump, "I'll show you your room. It's
called the Saturday bedroom and it's really
great. I have to share it with Araminta but *you*
can have it all to yourself."

Max did not look convinced. He kept staring at me, and the more Wanda pulled him up
the stairs, the more he hung back. I could see
his point because who would want to be
dragged anywhere by Wanda Wizzard? But
Wanda kept on tugging.

"Don't take any notice of Araminta—she's

~65~

always making faces," she told him in a loud voice while she stared right at me. "If she's not careful, the wind will change and she will get stuck like that. Not that you'd notice." Then she gave Max an extra-strong tug. Max gave in and they disappeared up the stairs.

So guess who had to carry the trunk all the way up to the Saturday bedroom? That's right, Uncle Drac and I. Of course it wouldn't fit up the rope ladder and through the little door at the top, so I let Wanda spend the rest of the afternoon climbing up and down the ladder with Max's stuff, which was good for her, as she has gained a bit of weight recently.

While Wanda was climbing up and down the ladder, I did some thinking. I had wondered how Pusskins was still managing to eat my cheese and onion crisps even when she had disappeared. But it was obvious now that I thought about it. It wasn't Pusskins who had been eating them, and it never had been. *It was the werewolf.*

So if I wanted to ever eat cheese and onion crisps again, there was a whole lot of stuff I had to do. And number one on the list was to get together a Werewolf Trapping Kit.

BATS

The trouble with collecting any kind of trapping kit is that sometimes someone traps *you* while you are doing it. And that is what happened: Barry made me help him take all the bat poo sacks out to the front gate. I do not know why people want to buy bat poo but they do. Barry says it is due to strategic advertising, which is what he calls the sign he sticks on top of the sacks that says:

guaranteed premium
ORGANIC BAT FERTILISER
made especially for you
by happy bats

When I asked Barry how he knew that the bats were happy, Barry said that he hadn't heard any of them saying they were *un*happy and that was good enough for him.

The rain had stopped while we were dragging out the sacks, but as we heaved the last one up against the hedge there was a sudden clap of thunder and the front door flew open with a bang. Great-aunt Emilene was standing on the top of the steps with Mathilda beside her. Right behind them I could see Aunt Tabby darting back and forth like a goalkeeper, making sure Great-aunt Emilene couldn't get back in.

"Good-bye, Mother," said Aunt Tabby in the extra-polite telephone voice she uses when she means the exact opposite of what she is saying. "It has been *so* nice to see you. *Do* come again. And don't worry about Maximilian, his little problem won't bother us. After all, ha-ha, we're used to *Araminta*."

I was glad that Great-aunt Emilene did not find this funny. She just glared at Aunt Tabby, then she threw the dead double ferret around her neck so fast that you could hear its glass eyes click together as she tottered off down the steps. Mathilda followed her and the skeleton Perkins jumped out of the car and held the door open for them. They drove off.

I was sad that Mathilda was going. I wouldn't have minded at all if *she* had stayed. As the hearse drove slowly past Barry and me, Great-aunt Emilene stared straight ahead like a statue, but Mathilda looked out of the window and waved. It was a small wave. I waved back.

They had not got far when the hearse came to halt and then started reversing down the lane. Aunt Tabby saw it coming. She slammed the front door with a bang, and I am sure I heard her bolting it and putting the chain on. *Great,* I thought. Mathilda has changed her mind and she is going to stay too. But it was

Perkins who got out. He didn't say a word. He just put some money for the bat poo in the box, heaved all the bat poo sacks into the back where the coffin had been, slammed the tailgate shut, and zoomed away.

"Strategic advertising," said Barry, sounding smug. "Always works."

Now that Barry had sold some poo he was in a good mood, so I said, "Barry, have you come across any werewolves around here?"

"Werewolves? Well, no. Although last year . . ."

"Did you find one last year?" I asked.

". . . I saw a really good film about them," he said.

"Oh. So nothing hiding underneath the bat poo then? Or creeping along behind you in the basement corridors?"

"No," said Barry, "because werewolves don't exist except in stories. Now Araminta, I'm going to fill some more sacks right away because it's not good for business to let the stock run out. That way you lose potential customers. Would you like to come and help?"

"No thank you, Barry," I said politely, since I knew he was trying to be nice. I wanted to ask him more about werewolves—like what *else* he thought could be hanging around staring at me with horrible flashing eyes, growling, and eating all my cheese and onion crisps—but I decided not to. Instead I would get my Werewolf Trapping Kit together, trap the werewolf, and then they would all *have* to believe me.

So for the next few days that is what I did. And it was a good thing I had something to do because my former best friend, Wanda Wizzard, was not my best friend any more. In fact she was more like my best "fiend", and I think she was haunting me. Everywhere I went I seemed to bump into her, and wherever she was, there was Max Spook, following her around like her own little puppy. Yuck. Clearly Wanda has no taste when it comes to friends—apart from me, of course. Which is, as Uncle Drac says, the exception that proves the rule.

First I found them in the ghost-in-the-bath bathroom, where Wanda was letting Max play with her acrobatic pet mice, which she never lets *me* touch. They had a whole mouse circus set up inside the haunted bath, which looked like fun.

Later I bumped into them in the long corridor that leads to the back door; Wanda was letting Max ride her new bike, which she won't let me near. He kept falling off and was obviously useless at riding a bike. But when Wanda saw me, did she say, "Oh, hello, Araminta, would you like a ride on my new bike too?" No, she did not. She said, "Oh, hello, Araminta, can Max borrow your skates?" Then she acted all shocked when I said, "No

way." Max just smiled a smug smile right at me and said, "Do not worry, Araminta. I do not like to skate."

When he smiled, he showed vampire teeth at the corners of his mouth! They were nothing like Uncle Drac's; they were *really* sharp, like little needles. In fact they were so sharp and pointy that they looked like the real thing—the *biting kind*.

I kept staring at Max, hoping for another look at his teeth, but he stopped smiling and stuck out his tongue at me. Then he fished a bag of sweets from his pocket and said, "*Wanda*, would you like a sweet?"

And Wanda said, "Ooh, yes *please*, Max. It is so lovely to have a friend who offers you sweets instead of eating them *all herself*."

I could have mentioned the gummi bears

but I did not. Max didn't offer me a sweet, but even if he had I wouldn't have taken it. Vampire sweets are not good. You should never take sweets from a vampire.

When Max wasn't being Wanda's puppy, he was being Aunt Tabby's creep.

That afternoon, Aunt Tabby decided to repaint the wood in the hall with thick, shiny brown paint, which was a nuisance since every time I walked through the hall collecting my Spooky Werewolf Trapping Kit I tripped over all kinds of painting stuff.

"Mind those tins of paint, Araminta," she snapped as I went past again.

"I was nowhere near those tins of paint," I said.

"You don't have to be *near* tins of paint for them to suddenly fall over, Araminta," she said, brushing her hair out of her eyes with painty hands. "They seem to take one look at you and throw themselves to the floor. Now, tell me, what do you think of the colour?"

"It's brown, Aunt Tabby," I said, trying to be helpful.

"Yes. But do you like it?"

I don't like brown. Not one bit. But I didn't

think I should say that. While I was thinking about what I *should* say, Max—who I am sure had been lurking in a dark corner and listening to every word—trotted up and said, "I *love* it. I think it is just the *perfect* shade of brown. You have a wonderful sense of colour, Aunt Tabitha."

Aunt Tabby smiled like he was the best thing in the world and then creepy Max said, "Please, may I clean your paint-brushes, Aunt Tabitha? I *love* to clean paintbrushes."

Aunt Tabby looked thrilled. "What a helpful boy

you are, Max," she purred. Then she looked at me in a less than thrilled way and said, "You see, Araminta, *that* is what I mean about being polite and helpful."

I left Aunt Tabby and Max discussing different shades of brown and got on with collecting the Spooky Werewolf Trapping Kit. And while I was doing that I was thinking about vampires.

This is what I was thinking: there are two kinds of vampires. There is the nice kind, like Uncle Drac, who does vampiry stuff like not liking daylight, hanging around with bats, and having cute pointy teeth at the sides of his smile. This is the kind of vampire who would not dream of biting you, not in a million years. They just happen to come from a vampire family, that is all. After all, some people say that I look like Aunt Tabby—which I *don't*—but even if I did, it wouldn't mean I actually acted like Aunt Tabby, would it? So you can look like a vampire but you don't have to behave like one.

Then there is the horrible kind of vampire. This is the nasty, biting kind whom you would not trust one inch. You can generally tell the nasty ones, as they are extremely creepy. They say nice things to people but they do not mean them. They lurk in corners listening to other people's conversations, they pretend that they are really helpful and considerate so that aunts love them, they steal people's best friends, *and they have really sharp teeth*. Does that remind you of anyone?

That's right: Max. *Vampire* Max.

It was obvious now: that was the reason

why Max was suddenly best friends with Wanda. Wanda is not easy to be best friends with—I should know. But Max didn't really want to be Wanda's friend; he wanted to *bite* her. And although I kind of thought it would serve Wanda right if she did get bitten, I didn't really want that to happen. That would make her a vampire too, and I didn't think Wanda would be a very good vampire. She would just be trouble. And she might bite *me*.

Something had to be done. The Spooky Werewolf Trapping Kit was now going to be the Spooky Combined Werewolf *and* Vampire Trapping Kit.

THE
TRAPPING KIT

By evening I had put together the best combined Werewolf and Vampire Trapping Kit ever.

It had:

* 1 bag of dog biscuits
* 1 extra-large fishing net
* 1 bat poo sack
* 1 long piece of rope
* 1 torch

✴ 1 roll of string (in case I had to go down any secret passages)

✴ 1 pencil and 1 piece of paper (in case I got trapped and had to write an SOS note)

✴ 1 pair of werewolf-eyes glasses

I am sure that there are lots of combined Werewolf and Vampire Trapping Kits around, but the werewolf-eyes glasses were what set the Spooky Trapping Kit above the rest. I made them from an old pair of Aunt Tabby's glasses that I had found in the back of an armchair and some hologram eyes from one of my last year's birthday cards. The birthday card had what was meant to be a cute little bunny on it, with cute little bunny eyes. But every time you looked at the bunny, its hologram eyes stared back and you got the creepy feeling that the bunny was watching you and waiting to pounce, because they were not cute bunny eyes at all—they were *werewolf* eyes. Someone in the card factory had stuck the wrong eyes on. I expect that somewhere there was a kid looking at a Halloween card that had a werewolf with cute bunny eyes thinking, 'Well, that's not at all scary; in fact I wouldn't mind one of those as a pet.'

I saved the card and when I was getting the Trapping Kit together I had the really great idea of making the glasses. So I stuck the werewolf-bunny hologram eyes on the glasses and put them on. I couldn't see much because Aunt Tabby's glasses make everything blurry anyway and the eyes kind of blanked everything else out, but I reckoned that in the dark

I could easily be mistaken for a werewolf. And that might come in handy on a werewolf vampire hunt, particularly as I reckoned there was a good chance that Vampire Max would be scared of werewolves.

Now I began to make plans. I was in the basement corridor working out the best place to spring the trap, when Wanda and Max came round the corner. They were so busy talking—and chewing sweets—that they didn't notice me.

"Come, Wanda," Max was saying, "you can show me the bat turret. I love to see bats."

I didn't like the sound of that. The bat turret is Uncle Drac's place, and the only people allowed in are me—of *course*—and Barry, who collects the bat poo. Horrible little vampires are most definitely *not* allowed.

Wanda trotted towards me and I stepped back into the doorway of the second-larder-on-the-left-just-past-the-boiler-room. She didn't see me. Max was following her, and as I watched him he took another sweet and bit into it with his pointy teeth, just as if he was doing a practice bite before biting Wanda. Wanda may not have been my best friend just then but I had to save her. So I jumped right out in front of them.

Wanda screamed. And then she saw it was me and she looked really annoyed. "Araminta, what are you doing here?" she asked.

"None of your business," I said. I could have told her that I was saving her from being bitten by a vampire but I didn't bother. I could tell that Wanda would not be grateful.

"Stop following us around," said Wanda.

"I am not following you around," I told her. "I have important business here."

"You *are* following us. Everywhere we go you are there, *lurking*," said Wanda, getting pink around the ears like she does when she is really fed up.

"*Me*, lurking?" I said, shocked. "It's not me who lurks. It's Vamp—it's Max who lurks."

Max didn't say anything. He just took another big sweet from his bag—a horrible blood-red piece this time—and shoved it into his mouth. I stared at his vampire teeth, wondering how come Wanda hadn't noticed them. Sometimes I think Wanda needs glasses.

"Come on, Max," said Wanda, taking Max's little stick-like arm. "*We* are going." And she stuck her nose in the air and stomped off back the way they came.

After that I decided that if Wanda wanted to get bitten by a vampire brat, then that was perfectly all right with me. The sooner the better, in fact. I carried on with my plans. I found a really great place to spring the werewolf trap, and then I took the Combined Werewolf and Vampire Trapping Kit up to our bedroom.

It was Saturday that day, but our bedroom was still the Friday bedroom since

You-Know-Who had stolen the best bedroom of the week. The Friday bedroom is OK though. It has a little arched window with a picture of a griffin on it that Sir Horace says came from his castle. It also has a very high, pointed ceiling; Wanda and I have our beds up on a platform close to the ceiling and you have to climb up a long ladder to get to them. If you want to get out of bed really quickly, there is a fireman's pole by *my* bed, and Wanda has to ask very nicely if she wants to use it. But just then Wanda could have asked as nicely as she wanted and I still would not have let her use it.

I like being on my own because I am used to it. Before Wanda came to live with us I spent lots of time on my own, so I was looking forward to just sitting on the griffin window seat and reading my book about were-wolves. I was sure that Wanda would still be with Max, but when I opened the door a little squeaky voice from far above said, "Hello, Araminta."

I did not answer.

"*Hello*, Araminta," Wanda said again.

"Oh, hello," I said in a bored voice. I picked up the *Werewolf Spotter's Handbook*, then I sat down under the griffin window and began to read it.

Wanda didn't say anything, but I knew she was looking at me and wanting me to stop reading. But I didn't. Then suddenly she blurted out, "He's a *vampire!*"

I did not answer. I am not that easily won over.

"Ara*min*ta," said Wanda, looking down at

me from her bed, her little legs swinging over the edge of the platform and her eyes almost popping out. "Maximilian is a *vampire*."

"I know," I said, sounding bored. I kept reading.

"You know? But *how*?" squeaked Wanda.

I shrugged, but I did not say anything.

Wanda did not say anything for a while either. She kept staring at me and trying to make me stop reading. But I would not give in. At last she gave up and said, "Araminta, can I slide down the fireman's pole?"

"No," I told her.

"Please?"

"No."

"I'll tell you all the vampiry things I have found out about Max. Can I? Please, please, *please*?"

"Oh, all right then."

"Great!" Wanda slid down the pole and a moment later she was beside me on the window seat under the griffin window saying "Budge up, Araminta" as she wriggled to get comfortable.

I closed my book. It was really nice to have Wanda sitting next to me although I wasn't going to let her know.

"I have discovered that Max is a *vampire*," Wanda said, her eyes almost popping out on to the floor.

"So?" I yawned.

"He talks just like vampires talk in films."

"I know," I said.

Wanda and I know all about vampire films because some nights, when we are supposed to be in bed, Uncle Drac sets up an old

projector in the furry bathroom—which is furry because of all the yucky green mould growing all over it—and Aunt Tabby watches old black-and-white vampire films and eats a ton of mint creams. Aunt Tabby thinks we are in bed—she does not know that Wanda and I are behind her sofa watching them too, *and* eating her mint creams when she is not looking.

"And he has really pointy teeth."

"I know," I said.

"And long scratchy nails."

"I know."

"And he *really* wanted to see the bats. But that isn't how I knew he was a vampire." Wanda wriggled even closer and whispered, "Araminta, do you want to know how I discovered that Max is a vampire?"

This was getting interesting. It sounded like Wanda had discovered something really bad. I nodded.

So Wanda whispered in my ear, "After you jumped out at us in the basement—"

"I did *not* jump out at you."

"Yes, you did. Anyway, after that we went to find some gummi bears, and one of the escaped bats flapped into us and *Max ate it*!"

That was horrible. "How did he eat it?" I asked. "Did he swallow it whole or chew it a bit first?"

"I don't know," said Wanda. "I didn't see."

"So how do you know for sure he ate it?"

"Because," Wanda whispered, "when we got into the kitchen he had *blood running down from the corners of his mouth*."

"Argh!" I dropped the *Werewolf Spotter's Handbook* on to the floor.

"Shhh, he'll hear you. Vampires have really good hearing," hissed Wanda. "Remember that movie where they tried to escape in the stagecoach along the top of that cliff in a thunderstorm but the vampire had heard all their plans and trapped them?"

I nodded again. I wished that I had seen the blood too as it sounded really fun—and it proved I was right about Max. "So while you were out vampiring with Vampire Max—" I said.

"I *wasn't* vampiring," Wanda interrupted.

"Well, while you were doing whatever with Max, *I* was busy putting together a Combined Werewolf and Vampire Trapping Kit," I said.

Wanda looked impressed. "You are so clever, Araminta."

"I know," I said.

As we were going down the stairs to supper, Wanda suddenly stopped and said, "But we don't *need* to trap Max, we know where he is. He will be downstairs having dinner with us."

I sighed. "But we have to trap him while he is biting someone, don't we? Otherwise Aunt Tabby will never believe it."

"Oh," said Wanda, "I see." And then she said in a worried voice, "But *who* will we trap him biting?"

Now when you are trapping vampires—or werewolves—you need one person to set the trap and another one to be bait. And since it was my trap, I would have to set it. Which, as far as I could see, left only one person who could be the bait. But I didn't tell Wanda that because I thought it might put her off her dinner. Despite what Aunt Tabby says, I think I can be quite thoughtful at times.

~8~

VAMPIRE STEW

Dinner that night was *weird*—and not just because the boiler exploded.

When Wanda and I got down to the second-kitchen-on-the-left-just-past-the-larder, Vampire Max was helping to lay the table and Aunt Tabby was saying, "Thank you, Maximilian dear, that is *so* helpful. And all the knives and forks are in the right places, too. You must show Araminta how to

lay the table so neatly."

Max simpered a smile, and I noticed he did not show Aunt Tabby his vampire teeth. He didn't look like a vampire at all; in fact he looked more like a freshly scrubbed teacher's pet. His hair was neatly combed, his face was shiny and pink—you could tell he had just washed it to get rid of the blood—and he had put on a *tie*. When Wanda and I arrived, he bowed. How creepy was *that*? But I could tell Aunt Tabby just thought it was good manners.

"Good evening, Vonda," he said, which is how he says Wanda's name. Wanda gave a kind of strangled yelp and scuttled off to her chair. "Good evening, Cousin Araminta," he said in my direction, and he bowed again.

Wanda was right—Max did have a creepy,

vampiry accent. Sometimes I notice that Uncle Drac has a bit of an accent like that but most of the time I don't notice it because I am used to Uncle Drac and he is not creepy at all.

"Say good evening to your cousin, Araminta," Aunt Tabby said. "And you can sit down and stop gaping too—it's rude to stare." She began to ladle a big pot of Aunt Tabby stew into our bowls. Wanda sighed. She does not like Aunt Tabby's cooking. I used to not mind it but Wanda's mum, Brenda, is a

much better cook and she usually makes din-
ners. But I supposed that she was still looking
for Pusskins.

"I am not gaping," I told Aunt Tabby. "Not
much stew for me, please."

Aunt Tabby took no notice. She ladled out
a huge scoop of gloop and
bits of it splattered down
my front. Yuck.

"You are not being
very polite, Araminta,"
said Aunt Tabby, annoyed,
as she ladled out an even bigger
pile of stew into Wanda's bowl.

"I must say, you could do worse than take a few tips from your Cousin Maximilian on manners. He is the politest and most considerate child I have ever met."

What was wrong with Aunt Tabby? Had she had a brain transplant or something? Couldn't she see how obvious it was that Max was the nasty, biting kind of vampire? I picked up my spoon and poked it at the stew, which felt kind of solid like a cube of jelly. Not a good sign.

Wanda was looking at her pile of stew as though it might be about to ambush her, but Vampire Max was wolfing his down and even managing to look like he was enjoying it. Aunt Tabby was gazing at him adoringly. I could see that Max could do no wrong in Aunt Tabby's eyes. Somehow I had to show Aunt Tabby what Vampire Max really was.

Suddenly I had a really brilliant idea. I had read somewhere that real vampires cannot bear to be near garlic. They hate the stuff. So, I decided to get him to give himself away. I stared really hard at him so that I did not miss a single flicker of expression, and I said very nicely, "Aunt Tabby, is there any garlic in this stew?"

"Garlic?" asked Aunt Tabby, looking puzzled.

Vampire Max looked up. *Aha.*

"Yes," I said, and I looked meaningfully at Vampire Max, "*garlic.*" Vampire Max did not react. He was stonewalling, I could tell.

"No, there isn't any garlic in it, Araminta." Aunt Tabby sounded touchy. "You don't like garlic."

"Yes I do. I really, *really* like garlic. Could

you grate some over it for me please?"

"What, *raw* garlic?" asked Aunt Tabby. "Are you *sure?*"

I nodded. It couldn't make the stew taste any worse and it was an important vampire test that had to be done. I glanced at Wanda and she looked very puzzled.

Aunt Tabby sighed, scraped her chair back, and got up. She came back with a big head of garlic and a little grater. It was the moment of truth. I stared at Vampire Max and he stared at the garlic like he couldn't believe what he was seeing. I knew I was getting somewhere.

Aunt Tabby got busy with the grater and dumped a whole load of garlic on top of my jelly-stew. Yuck. It smelled disgusting. Aunt Tabby is right, I do not like garlic one bit.

"Can you give some to Wanda too?" I asked.

"What, *me?*" squeaked Wanda.

"Yes, I don't want to be greedy and take it all," I said.

"I don't mind, Araminta, really I don't," said Wanda as Aunt Tabby got busy grating garlic all over her stew too.

"And I don't want to leave Vamp—I mean Max—out," I said to Aunt Tabby. "I am sure he would like some."

"No!" Vampire Max almost shouted. "I do not like garlic upon my stew. It is perfect as it is, thank you, Aunt Tabitha. I have never tasted a more delicious stew," he said, carefully smiling his no-teeth smile at Aunt Tabby.

"Oh, how kind of you to say that, Max," simpered Aunt Tabby. She sat down and began to cut up her stew with a knife and fork. "You could learn a lot from the way Maximilian behaves, Araminta," she said, fixing me with a beady glare.

It is always best to change the subject when Aunt Tabby is grumpy, so I quickly said, "Has Brenda found Pusskins yet?" but it didn't seem to work.

"No," snapped Aunt Tabby, and she cut up another mouthful of stew.

"Probably," I whispered to Wanda, "because it is *Pusskins* in the stew." Wanda gasped and dropped her spoon. Aunt Tabby—who says that whispering in front of other people is just about the rudest thing you can ever do—looked like she was going to explode.

But the boiler got there first—*bang!*

~9~

BOILER BRAT

The boiler room was an awful mess—it looked just like it used to before Brenda arrived, when Aunt Tabby took care of the boiler all on her own. There was soot everywhere, the boiler door was swinging from the lampshade, and there were pieces of boiler all around the room.

At the sound of her precious boiler exploding, Brenda had come running. She

took one look and screamed, "My boiler, my *boiler*!"

"It's not that bad, Brenda," said Aunt Tabby huffily, "I've seen worse." She handed Brenda a bucket. "Put the pieces in there and I'll fix it later."

Brenda snatched the bucket and glared at Aunt Tabby. "You will not fix it later," she said. "*I* will fix it *now*. Oh, *there's* a good boy, Max, how sweet of you. Thank you, dear," she said, beaming at You-Know-Who. Vampire Max had got hold of the broom, which was twice as big as he was, and was busy sweeping up all the soot.

Brenda glared at Wanda with a distinctly Aunt-Tabby-like expression. "*That*, Wanda," she said, "is what I mean by being helpful. Little Max didn't wait to be asked to sweep up, did he? He just got on and did it."

Wanda did not look impressed by this information. In fact she looked pretty annoyed. She grabbed hold of my sleeve and tugged me out of the boiler room, "Come on, Araminta," she said loudly. "Let's go. You can have some of my gummi bears."

We sat in the dark in the first-kitchen-on-the-left-just-by-the-stairs, which is where

Wanda keeps her gummi bear stash, and ate two whole bags between us. It was fun, just like old times before Vampire Max arrived. No one guessed we were there.

We were just wondering whether to share a third bag of bears when who should come past but Brenda and Aunt Tabby—with Vampire Max trotting between them like a little dog. Both of them were cooing over him.

"It was so *sweet* of you to help me fix the boiler, Max," said Brenda. "I have tried to get Wanda to show an interest in the boiler but she really does not care."

"But boilers are *fascinating*, Mrs Wizzard," said Max in his creepy voice.

Brenda giggled. "Oh Max dear, you must call me Brenda. All my friends do. And I do hope we are friends."

Wanda made her sick-bag face at me. I made one back.

Aunt Tabby was just as bad. "I think you have earned a little treat, Maximilian. Do you like mint creams?"

"They are my *favourite*, Aunt Tabitha," said creepy Max.

Well. Aunt Tabby never offers *me* any of her precious mint creams.

We waited until the Vampire Max fan club had gone and then we crept into the basement corridor, which was really dark because all the lights had gone out when the boiler exploded.

Suddenly I saw the werewolf eyes again— and they were staring right at us. They were really close to the ground this time, and I knew that meant only one thing—that the werewolf was about to pounce. I grabbed Wanda's arm.

"Ouch!" she yelped.

"Shh . . . werewolf!" I hissed. But as soon as I spoke the eyes disappeared back into the darkness.

"*I* didn't see it," said Wanda.

"It *was* the werewolf. What else has staring eyes and lopes around in the dark?"

We had reached the foot of the stairs that go up from the basement and I could see Wanda's face now in the light coming down from the hall. She had on her I-don't-believe-you expression. "It wasn't loping, Araminta," she said. "If it had been *loping* we would have heard it."

"So what exactly does loping sound like?" I asked Miss Know-It-All.

"Sort of scuffling, like this"—Wanda scraped her shoes along the floor—"and then kind of dragging, like this," and she did a weird walk like a crab short of a few legs.

"Pwfeeergh!" I snorted.

"It's not funny," said Wanda.

"Yes . . . it *is*." It was no good. I had the giggles. I sat down on the stairs and choked and spluttered while Wanda looked cross. She stood tapping her little foot, waiting for me to stop, and then suddenly she shrieked, "Look, look! Werewolf paw prints!"

She was right. All along the corridor were big sooty werewolf paw prints—and they were heading upstairs. *The werewolf was loose in Spook House.*

"Run!" I yelled. And we did. We both ran as fast as we could and we did not stop until we reached our Friday bedroom. And Wanda didn't even stop then—she scooted up the ladder to her bed and dived under the blankets. I slammed the bedroom door behind me and shoved a chair up underneath the handle like the heroine always does in films when the vampire has chased her through his castle at midnight and cornered her in some deserted room—far away from all her silly friends, who have no idea at all what is going on. I waited for the door handle to rattle like it does when the vampire tries the door and you just *know* she's in for it and is about to become vampire fodder—but it didn't. We were safe.

Well, not exactly *safe*, as we had a vampire and a werewolf wandering around Spook House—but that was OK because I had a

Plan. The trouble with my Plan was that I needed Wanda's help, and Wanda was under the bedclothes trembling like a great big jelly. So while Wanda was doing her jelly impression I checked my Combined Werewolf and Vampire Trapping Kit. It was all there.

I pulled Wanda out of bed to show her what was definitely the best Combined Werewolf and Vampire Trapping Kit *ever*. "This is going to be the best Combined Werewolf and Vampire Trapping Expedition ever," I told her. "Obviously we will have to wait until midnight because that is the time when you can be sure to find both vampires *and* were-wolves hanging around. But I am sure it won't take long to trap them both."

"I am *not* going on a Combined Werewolf

and Vampire Trapping Expedition, Araminta," she said. "No *way*. Especially not at midnight. I wouldn't go *anywhere* in Spook House at midnight."

Wanda is such a spoilsport. "If it wasn't at midnight would you go?" I asked.

"No."

I felt really fed up. It takes two people *minimum* to catch a vampire or a werewolf. One person has to be the bait—which, as I have said, was ideal for Wanda—and the other one has to have split-second timing and lightning-fast reactions—which I could easily do. But obviously I could not do both at once.

There was no one else I could ask either. Grown-ups are absolutely no use at stuff like that, which ruled out Brenda, Barry, Uncle Drac, and Aunt Tabby—and who would want

Aunt Tabby helping them catch vampires and werewolves at midnight anyway? She would frighten them away. Ghosts would be no good at that sort of stuff because generally they cannot hold anything, and our particular kinds of ghosts would definitely be of no help—Sir Horace would just fall to pieces and Edmund would be even more scared than Wanda. The only other person in Spook House who would have been OK was Max— except it was *him* that we needed to catch.

It was dark now and I sat on the griffin window seat and watched a brilliant full moon slowly rise above the trees at the end of the garden. It was a perfect night for a Combined Werewolf and Vampire Trapping Expedition, but right then the best chance the Combined Werewolf and Vampire Trapping

Kit had of working was for me to chuck it out of the window in the hope that it would hit one of them on the head.

But, you know, sometimes things do work out in the most unexpected way. A few minutes later the Friday bedroom door began to glow with a strange green light. I was so surprised that I nearly joined Wanda under the blankets.

I was halfway up the ladder when I realised it was only Edmund. He shimmered through the door and kind of floated just above the floor. Edmund is quite a small ghost, although he is probably about ten, but I think kids were smaller in medieval times, which is when he is from. He has a pudding-basin haircut, wears a tunic, and has an old dagger tucked into his belt. He talks with a funny accent and

Sir Horace says that
is because he lived
in somewhere called
Normandy before he
became Sir Horace's page.
Edmund was only seven when
he left home and went to live in Sir
Horace's castle, which is very young to start
work. I guess that might excuse him for being
so weedy—but it is still irritating.

"What do you want, Edmund?" I asked.

I felt annoyed at being halfway up the
ladder like I was scared or something, and

even more annoyed when Wanda poked her head out from under the blankets and said, "Oh, hello, Edmund," in an excited, really-happy-to-see-him kind of voice. She never sounds like that when she sees *me*.

"Sir Horace has sent me," he said. **"He seeks your help."**

Now this sounded interesting.

"What kind of help?" asked Wanda, who is nosy and always asks questions.

"I cannot say, Wanda. I am but the messenger. He asks that you meet him at his treasure chest at midnight."

"OK," I said. "I'll meet him, but Wanda won't because she doesn't like going out at midnight."

"Yes I do," said Wanda. "I *love* going out at

midnight. You can tell Sir Horace that we'll both come, Edmund."

Well.

The Combined Werewolf and Vampire Trapping Expedition was *on*.

~10~

VAMPIRE HUNT

Wanda could not stay awake. Soon she was snuffling away like a hedgehog, which is how she always sounds when she sleeps. So I had to stay awake to make sure we were down in the hall at midnight. I sat in bed and finished the *Werewolf Spotter's Handbook*. Then I started reading *Vampire Trapping for Beginners*, which was OK but a bit boring because it seemed you had to be a German

professor with a funny name before you had any hope of catching a vampire. My eyes began to feel very sleepy and kept closing, and I had to keep jumping awake again. It was very annoying, since I really didn't want to miss midnight.

To try and stay awake I listened to all the night-time noises. Most people would find it really spooky in Spook House at night, as there are all kinds of weird sounds, but I do not find it spooky at all because I know what they all are.

Most of the noises are made by Uncle Drac. Uncle Drac spends a lot of the day asleep in his sleeping bag in the bat turret, which means he wanders around Spook House in the night. But I know Uncle Drac's grumbly cough and the sound of his footsteps, and I like to hear him padding about. Aunt Tabby does not sleep well and she often gets up and goes all the way down to the kitchen to make a cup of tea. I know her footsteps too; they are kind of impatient and spiky. Recently she has been watching vampire films in the furry bathroom so I sometimes hear the whirr of the projector and the clattering sound the film makes when it comes to the end of a reel.

Brenda and Barry do not walk around Spook House at night at all. No way. Although Brenda pretends that she is not afraid of the dark, I know she is. And I also know that she locks the door of their big bedroom at the front of the house and makes Barry stay with her. He is not allowed to go out for even one moment, just in case the monster statue outside their window comes alive and bites them. Well, that's what Wanda said and she should know.

There are other things that make nighttime noises in Spook House. There is Sir Horace—who rattles when he walks, which is a bit of a giveaway; there are the hot water pipes, which gurgle; the big floorboards on the landing that creak as the house cools down; the grandfather clock in the hall, which has the loudest tick you can imagine and—ever since Aunt Tabby tried to fix it— chimes thirteen times every hour; and the family of rats that chase each other all around the attic and sound like they are wearing hiking boots.

So if you stayed the night in Spook House I guess you might spend a lot of it lying awake and listening to everything, just like Wanda did when she first came. But if you stayed for a few more nights you would soon get used to it and end up snuffling like a hedgehog just like Wanda. Except *no one* snuffles like Wanda.

The clock in the hall had just chimed thirteen again and I opened my eyes with a jolt. I didn't *think* I had been asleep and I reckoned that it was now eleven o'clock. So I listened to the Spook House sounds, and everything was surprisingly quiet, apart from the odd creak from the floorboards on the landing. And then I heard a new sound . . .

First I heard the sound of a door opening, but it was not Aunt Tabby's door or the door to Uncle Drac's turret—it was the door to our Saturday bedroom. I knew that because it has a particular sound, kind of an ooooooh-ah-*eeeeek*. Then I heard a soft creak-thump-creak-thump, and I realised it was the sound that the rope ladder makes when someone climbs down it. And at once I knew who that must be—*Vampire Max*.

I shot up to the snuffling hedgehog and shook her awake. *"Wandaaaaaaa!"* I hissed right in her ear. Wanda sat up with her hair sticking out on end like she had had an electric shock.

"Wherrr?"

"Vampire Max—he's out vampiring. I can *hear* him."

"Eer?"

"Come on, Wanda. Hurry *up*."

The trouble with hedgehogs is they do not like waking up. I had to drag Wanda out of bed and make her feet walk down the ladder, which was not easy, but I did it. Soon she was standing by the Combined Werewolf and Vampire Trapping Kit in her yucky sweet-dreams-pink-fairy pyjamas, rubbing her eyes. "Is it morning?' she mumbled.

"No," I said. "Put your slippers on and follow me."

I don't think Wanda had figured out what we were doing, but she put on her fluffy rabbit slippers with the silly ears while I heaved the Combined Werewolf and Vampire Trapping Kit over my shoulder. I think it was only when we got outside our bedroom that Wanda really woke up. Her eyes popped wide open and she stared around as if she was really surprised at where she was. I am sure she would have squeaked out loud if I hadn't shoved my hand over her mouth.

"Wrrrrer!" she gasped.

I put my finger to my lips and beckoned her to follow me, which she did. We hid in the shadows and crept along the wide passageway that runs along the back of the attic, where all the doors to the days-of-the-week bedrooms are. Wanda is quite good at creeping and so am I, since I have had lots of practice creeping up on Aunt Tabby when she is not looking, so it was easy for us to get really close to our Saturday bedroom rope ladder. And sure enough, there he was: Vampire Max was climbing down the ladder like a little black spider.

A bright shaft of moonlight was shining on to the ladder and as Vampire Max stepped off, it shone on to his pasty white face and glinted on his slicked-back hair. He was wearing black pyjamas and a weird black velvet jacket tied with a silk cord. He looked just like a mini vampire from one of Aunt Tabby's films.

Wanda was wide awake now. Her fingers were digging into my arm and they really hurt, but I had to keep quiet because this was a real-life Combined Vampire and Werewolf Trapping Expedition. And the vampire part was already up and running.

Vampire Max walked off along the attic corridor and then started down the stairs, with the intrepid Professor Von Spook and her gullible but well-meaning sidekick following close behind. He didn't notice a thing. There was a tricky moment when Wanda walked through a big spider's web and I thought she was going to yell, but she didn't. We followed Vampire Max down the attic stairs and then we set off along the landing, keeping to the shadows and away from the really creaky floorboards. It was weird, but fun in a spooky kind of way.

In Spook House there are lots of doors and winding passageways that go to bedrooms and bathrooms and turrets and all kinds of places. We walked along the passage that went past the furry bathroom and I could see the flickering light of the film streaking out of the half-open door. As we crept by I glanced in and saw Aunt Tabby's head silhouetted against the light from the projector. Her head had a very strange shape because she wears great big headphones so that the noise does not bother anyone. This was good because there was no chance that she could hear us creeping by—even when Wanda trod on a creaky floorboard and we had to dive into the shadows in case Vampire Max turned around. But he didn't. He just kept moving, his little legs walking in that creepy vampiry way of his, as if he knew exactly where he was going.

It is quite easy to get lost in Spook House, especially at night. There are dead-end passages, stairs that go nowhere, and all kinds of zigzag corridors that go around in circles and make you confused. There are also tons of mouldy curtains that hang around the place and jump out on you when you are least expecting it, and *that* was how we lost Vampire Max. One minute we were tailing him along the twisty passageway in the west wing that goes to the locked turret, and the next moment a horrible dusty curtain had flopped in front of us, and Wanda was covered in a flock of moths.

"Ugh!" yelped Wanda.

"Shhh!" I hissed, and pulled her back behind the curtain. Everybody knows that the most important thing about a vampire hunt is that they must not know you are hunting them, otherwise they can get very nasty indeed, and I was afraid that Vampire Max would hear us. We hid behind the smelly old curtain listening for his footsteps coming back towards us, but we heard nothing. Very carefully, I pulled the curtain back, half expecting to see Max staring at us with his little beady eyes and blood dripping from his mouth—but there was no sign of him. We had lost him.

But Wanda did not care. She yawned and said, "Let's catch him tomorrow then. I'm *really* sleepy, I want to go back to bed."

"You can't," I told her. "It will be midnight

soon, which is when we promised Edmund that we would meet Sir Horace at his treasure chest. Remember?"

"Oh," said Wanda.

There was no sign of Sir Horace in the ghost-in-the-bath bathroom. After what felt like a few centuries I asked Wanda what time it was, since I do not have a watch.

Wanda always wears her pink fairy watch. She says that Pusskins gave it to her for her birthday, which is obviously not true because cats cannot give birthday presents, and even if they could I do not think that cats would *bother* to give birthday presents—especially a grumpy cat like Pusskins. But on the card it had said *Happy Birthday, Wanda. Love from Pusskins xxx*, and that is what Wanda believes. On the watch is a prancing fairy, and instead of regular watch hands the fairy's wings go round. Wanda was squinting at the wings for ages trying to work out what the time was, so I took a look. It was hard to tell, but it looked like one wing was straight up, and the other one nearly was too. I reckoned it must be almost midnight.

Wanda started up again about going back to bed.

"No," I told Wanda very firmly, "you are *not* going back to bed. We are on a Combined Werewolf and Vampire Trapping Expedition and we haven't even finished the *first* half of it since we have not found a single werewolf, let alone trapped the vampire."

"I don't care," said Wanda grumpily. "I don't want to find a single werewolf. I don't even want to find a double werewolf. I don't care about vampires. I want to go back to bed."

"All right, go back to bed then. *I'm* waiting for Sir Horace. I'll see you later," I said.

Wanda stared at me like I'd said something really dumb. "I'm not going back on my *own*, Araminta," she said.

At that moment I heard the telltale clank of Sir Horace's armour.

"Ah, Miss Spook and Miss Wizzard. Thank you for meeting me here. It is most kind," Sir Horace boomed as he walked into the ghost-in-the-bath bathroom.

"It's a pleasure, Sir Horace," Wanda piped up, conveniently forgetting that a few seconds earlier she had been about to bunk off to bed and desert Sir Horace.

"How kind of you, Miss Wizzard. It is always

a pleasure to meet you, and Miss Spook, too," said Sir Horace.

I didn't want to hang around too long with Sir Horace, as we still had a vampire and a werewolf to catch and time was getting on, so I asked, "Why did you want to see us, Sir Horace?"

"I would be most grateful if you would do me a favour, Miss Spook. Would you be so kind as to open my treasure chest for me?"

I wondered why Sir Horace needed us to open the chest at midnight, seeing as he could have asked us any old time of day, but I didn't say anything. I lifted up the lid. "There you are Sir Horace," I said. "We'll be off now."

"Could I trouble you to do me one more favour before you go, Miss Spook? Would you be so kind as to take out the small silver whistle and blow three times, just as the clock chimes the hour?"

This sounded very mysterious. I scrabbled around in the chest and found the whistle. It looked very small and scratched.

"Ah," said Sir Horace when he saw the whistle. "There it is. Those were happy days. I remember when Fang would—" At that moment the clock in the hall began to chime thirteen and Sir Horace almost yelled, "Blow! Blow the whistle, Miss Spook."

So I did. Well, I think I did. I blew a big puff of air into it but no sound came out. I blew again. And then one last time, which made three. Sir Horace did not seem worried that the whistle made no noise.

"Thank you so much, Miss Spook," he said. "Now I must be off to await my faithful Fang."

He spun around on his foot and almost ran out of the ghost-in-the-bath bathroom.

"Who's Fang?" whispered Wanda, sounding scared.

"I think it was his dog," I said, trying to remember what Sir Horace had told me on the stairs. "Shh—what's that?"

We shrank back into the bathroom just in time—and who should walk by but Vampire Max?

~11~

BAIT

The Combined Werewolf and Vampire Trapping Expedition was back on track—at least the vampire part was.

I beckoned to Wanda. She sighed and mouthed, "Do we *have* to?" and I mouthed back, "Yes!"

We crept out of the ghost-in-the-bath bathroom and followed Max. This time I was determined not to lose him so I

got as close as I dared.

I guess I was a bit jumpy by now because I caught sight of something moving along the floor beside me and I nearly yelled, but then I realised that it was only the stupid shiny ears on Wanda's slippers waggling as she tiptoed along.

Max headed into the twisty corridor that led to the locked turret. I know it really well since before Wanda came to live here I used to spend a lot of time trying to pick the lock. I wondered if maybe Max had a key! Maybe the turret was stuffed full of vampires and he hadn't really come to stay with us at all—he had come to stay with *them*.

Max wandered round another corner in the corridor, and I tried to make Wanda speed up a bit. She was dragging her rabbit slippers and was not exactly the enthusiastic assistant a vampire hunter needs. So I was not surprised that when we eventually got round the next corner, Max was gone.

I could see the steps leading to the locked turret and the big cobwebby door at the top of them—but no Max. Not a good sign. I rushed up the steps and tried the door, but it was locked as usual, and I could tell it had not been opened as it was covered in very old and dusty spiders that looked like they had not moved in years.

It was weird. Vampire Max had completely disappeared—just like in the movie where the vampire suddenly falls through a trapdoor into the river below and *dissolves*. But as much as I hoped that Max had fallen through a trapdoor and dissolved, I knew he couldn't have.

I know where all the trapdoors are in Spook House, and there definitely is not one in the twisty corridor to the locked turret.

So where *was* he?

And then I remembered. The locked turret has a fire escape chute! Underneath the steps is a little red door, just like the one that goes into Uncle Drac's bat turret—except this door leads to a big tube that runs all the way around the locked turret and takes you right down to the basement. I hadn't gone down it since I was little because Aunt Tabby had told me not to, and despite what you may think, I do sometimes take notice of what Aunt Tabby says. She also told me that a scary monster lived inside it, so that put me off a bit too. But now I was big enough to know that Aunt Tabby was fibbing about the monster.

Wanda did not want to go down the fire escape chute—and especially not when I opened the little door and shone my torch into it, for it was stuffed full of spiders' webs.

"I am not going down there, Araminta," she said. "No way."

I could tell from the way she said it she would not change her mind, so I pushed her in and jumped in after her. It was *great*. Wanda screamed a bit but that was OK, as all the spiders' webs muffled the sound. We rocketed down, round and round, but I didn't get a bit dizzy, and in no time we shot out into an old larder in the basement.

Wanda did not appreciate it. Especially when I landed right on top of her. She jumped up and I could see she was about to yell at me,

so I put my hand over her mouth and hissed, "Shh!"

I switched on my torch. Wanda looked really funny; she was *covered* in cobwebs, dust, and spiders. I was not as bad since Wanda had acted like a chimney sweep's brush, so I only had a few spiders wandering around my hair, which was OK.

I was surprised that Wanda was not making more of a fuss, like she usually does, but she was staring at the floor. "Araminta," she whispered, "there's . . . werewolf stuff."

For a moment I did not want to look, as I thought it might be something really gross, like werewolf poo, but I did. A trapper of werewolves has to face these things. But it was worse than werewolf poo—it was *werewolf footprints*. There were tons of them. They went round and round in circles inside the larder and then they zigzagged out the door and disappeared along the corridor. The werewolf had gone back to its lair.

I wasn't quite as pleased about this as I should have been.

"You're shaking," said Wanda.

"No I'm not," I said. "Your eyes must be going funny."

Now we *had* to set the werewolf trap. I had already worked out the perfect place for it— a tall, thin cupboard just past the bat poo hatch where Uncle Drac used to store his shovels. I knew there was enough room in it for Wanda because I had once locked her in there by mistake—it really *was* a mistake, even though Aunt Tabby would not believe me, but the day before I had checked that there was enough room for me, which there was. There was not space for us both but that was OK since Wanda was not going to be inside the cupboard. She had a very important job to do outside. She was going to be the bait.

I beckoned Wanda out of the larder, then I switched off my torch because I did not want the werewolf to see us. It was really scary, as we tiptoed along the creepy basement corridor, past all the dark kitchens and the deserted larders and pantries. Even the boiler room was scary with its dull red glow seeping out from underneath the door, and the funny breathing sounds the boiler made, like it was a sleeping monster.

Soon we were really close to Creepy Corner, where I had seen the werewolf eyes.

We tiptoed past the bat poo hatch and stopped outside Uncle Drac's old shovel cupboard. I wanted to get into that cupboard fast. I hadn't told Wanda about being the bait yet, because I thought it would probably lead to trouble. So I just gave her the bag of dog biscuits, then opened the cupboard door and got inside.

I was about to shut the door when I noticed Wanda looking at the dog biscuits in a puzzled way. "Ugh," she said, "these biscuits smell funny. *You* can have them, Araminta."

"They're supposed to smell funny. They're *dog* biscuits," I explained. "They're going to help us catch the werewolf."

Wanda looked puzzled. "So why

am *I* holding them?" she asked.

I sighed. It is hard having to explain stuff all the time, especially when a werewolf might pounce at any moment. "Because you are the bait," I told her.

"Bait?" Wanda's eyes almost popped out. "No *way*," she said. "Let me into the cupboard."

"Don't be silly, Wanda," I told her. "There isn't enough room for two of us."

Wanda seemed to take this in. She looked at the cupboard and said, "No, there isn't, is there?" The next moment she had pulled me out of the cupboard, pushed the dog biscuits into my hands, jumped in herself, and slammed the door shut.

I pulled on the cupboard door but it would not open. I could tell that Wanda was holding it closed from the inside. So there I was, in a deserted corridor in the middle of the night, holding a bag of dog biscuits and waiting for the nearest werewolf to pounce at any moment. It was not a good feeling.

I felt like banging on the door, and yelling "*Let me in*," but I dared not make any noise in case the werewolf heard. There was nothing else to do—it was time to use the Combined Werewolf and Vampire Trapping Kit.

I got the fishing net out fast, just in case the werewolf came zooming around the corner right then, and I practised a few swoops with it. It worked fine. Then I took out both of the sacks and the rope.

And then I pulled out the best part of the kit—the werewolf-eyes glasses. I put them on. Pooh. I couldn't see—the stickers were in the way. I hadn't thought of that. But then I realised that the hologram werewolf eyes did not have to be over my eyes, they could be *anywhere*. So I pushed the glasses up on to my forehead and they were fine. Now I was ready for anything: vampires, werewolves, even Aunt Tabby.

But I wasn't quite ready for the scuffling. I do not like scuffling, especially when it is after midnight in the basement of Spook House and my so-called best friend has locked herself in a cupboard and left me outside as werewolf bait. At first I hoped it might be one of Uncle Drac's bats. When Barry shovels up the bat poo some of the bats get out and he does not notice. But bats do not scuffle along the ground. The scuffling was getting closer . . . and closer. I shrank back against the wall and I must have done a Wanda-style squeak or something because suddenly the cupboard door opened behind me. I nearly screamed.

Wanda stuck her nosy nose out and whispered, "Are you all right, Araminta?'

"No," I told her.

"Why? What is it?"

"What do you think it is? There's a *werewolf* coming. Can't you hear it?"

Wanda listened. Scuffle . . . scuffle . . . She went kind of pale. "Get in the cupboard," she hissed, and she grabbed hold of my sleeve and tugged me in. I didn't think we'd both fit, but it is surprising how small you can make yourself when you have to. Wanda pulled the door closed. It wouldn't click shut properly, but she held it so that it stayed closed and then we both kept really quiet . . . and listened.

Scuffle . . . sniff . . . scuffle . . . sniff. The werewolf was really loud now. It was right outside the cupboard. It snuffled a bit, sniffed a bit, and rustled the dog biscuit bag. And then it started to scratch on the cupboard door, which would have been all right if at that point Wanda hadn't decided for some crazy reason to try and burrow into the back of the cupboard. Suddenly there was nothing behind us—and we both fell backwards into the dark.

~12~

FANG

I landed on top of Wanda, which was OK as Wanda is quite soft to land on. I looked up and saw the high brick roof of the secret tunnel that runs through the basement and I felt really relieved—we were safe. But then I saw the werewolf eyes. *And this time they were right above me.*

It was too late to ask Wanda to swap places so I just yelled "Help!" and Wanda kind of

squeaked. The werewolf eyes got closer and I realised that these were different werewolf eyes. They glinted silver, not green, and they looked much, *much* bigger. This was bad. And what was worse, I did not even have my Combined Werewolf and Vampire Trapping Kit with me—just when I needed it.

The only thing to do was to make a run for it. Just as I was wondering if I should take Wanda with me or leave her behind as bait, a greenish glow began to light up the tunnel.

Suddenly Edmund's ghostly voice said, "What are *you* doing here?"

"Edmund!" squeaked Wanda. She wriggled out from underneath me and jumped up. "Oh, Edmund, you've *saved* us," she said as if he was some kind of hero. Which he was *not*, since he hadn't saved us at all.

The glow from Edmund meant I could see the werewolf very well. It was a huge wolf and it was *horrible*. Its mouth was hanging open, its tongue was lolling out, and its great big fangs were ready to bite us.

And what could a weedy ghost do about that?

Well, what the weedy ghost did was to go up to the werewolf, scratch its ears and say, **"Hello, Fang, where have you been?"** And the werewolf sat down and wagged its tail just like a dog.

"Oh, Edmund," said Wanda dreamily, "you are so *brave*."

"I am not brave, Wanda," Edmund said in his funny accent. **"Now I must go and find Sir Horace. I shall return soon."**

"Edmund," wailed Wanda, "don't leave us with a werewolf."

Edmund laughed. At least that's what I think the weird noise he made was meant to be. **"Fang is not a werewolf,"** he said. **"Fang is Sir Horace's faithful wolf cub."** And then he floated away and left us alone—with Fang.

"Shall I say hello to Fang too?' whispered Wanda, who would copy everything Edmund did if she could, although I think she would find it hard to float upside down along the ceiling.

"If you want to," I said.

"Fang is so nice," she said. "He's got such soft ears."

"How can you possibly know that?" I asked. "He's a *ghost*."

"I just do know that," said Wanda, busily scratching thin air. "You can tell they would be soft if he was a real wolf."

"If he was a real wolf you would *not* be scratching his ears," I told her. "You would be wolf supper."

It was not long before we heard the eek-squeak-clunk of Sir Horace walking along the secret passage and the walls were lit up with Edmund's green glow. Sir Horace came around the corner and then he suddenly stopped dead. There was a small *ping* as something fell off him, and I held my breath in case he fell apart, but he didn't.

Suddenly the secret passage was filled with a booming, happy Sir Horace voice, *"Fang!"*

Fang leaped up, leaving Wanda actually scratching thin air. He bounced over to Sir Horace like a huge puppy, his tail wagging and his tongue hanging out. Sir Horace knelt down—with a nasty grinding noise and an ominous clunk—and he put his rusty old arms around Fang. **"Hello, boy,"** he said in a whispery un-Sir-Horace-like voice. **"Where have *you* been then?"**

"Ooh, that's so nice," cooed Wanda. "Isn't

it, Edmund?" She didn't ask me if it was nice because I am not as soppy as Edmund. But it was. Really great.

Sir Horace's booming voice still had a big smile in it when he said, **"Miss Spook, I have you to thank for the return of my faithful hound. Your midnight summons has brought him once more to my side."**

"It's a pleasure, Sir Horace," I said. "Anytime. Come on, Wanda."

"But I want to stay with Fang," she said, ruffling the ghost wolf's ears. "He's *so* cute."

"You can see Fang later," I told her. "In case you had forgotten we are still on a Combined Werewolf and Vampire Hunt. Come *on*."

We left Sir Horace with his faithful wolf and walked back through Uncle Drac's cupboard—which was, of course, the hidden door into the secret tunnel that I always knew must be somewhere.

"Now that we have found the werewolf, can we go back to bed?" asked Wanda.

I picked up my Combined Werewolf and Vampire Trapping Kit from where it had fallen. "No, we cannot go back to bed, Wanda," I said sternly. "We have not found the werewolf, we have found a ghost wolf. A ghost wolf would not leave footprints, would it? And the werewolf had green eyes, not silver ghostly eyes. And have you forgotten about Vampire Max?"

Wanda did not reply. At first I thought she was being sulky, as Wanda does big sulks, but she grabbed me and pointed to the bat poo hatch. It was open.

Inside the bat turret there was a flickering light and bat shadows flying across the old stone walls. I don't mind bat shadows, since they are made by bats and bats are nice, but I don't like scary shadows. And I particularly don't like big scary shadows of *werewolves*. And there was a *huge* one of those inside the bat turret. Suddenly the Combined Werewolf and Vampire Trapping Kit didn't feel so great after all—not even my werewolf-eyes glasses.

I pulled Wanda away, but it was too late. The werewolf shadow had seen us and it was coming toward us. I could hear the soft squelching sounds that footsteps make in the bat poo.

"Run!" I yelled to Wanda, who didn't seem to want to. "Come *on*!" The shadow was coming closer.

I gave Wanda a massive tug and she lurched forward. "Ouch!" she yelled. "Don't *pull*,

Araminta, it's only U—"

Suddenly I heard "Minty? Minty, is that you?"

"Uncle Drac!" I shouted. "I am *so* pleased to see you!"

"I *told* you," muttered Wanda.

Uncle Drac squeezed out of the bat poo hatch holding his torch. He was carrying a big Werewolf-shaped sack of bat poo over his shoulder. He looked very surprised. "Goodness me, Minty, what *are* you doing here at this time of night?"

"We were hunting a werewolf, Uncle Drac."

"And a vampire, but he disappeared," Wanda piped up.

"Well, just don't go telling all that to Aunt Tabby," Uncle Drac said with a smile. "It's way past your bedtime. Come on, I'll take you both back upstairs."

I suppose I should have been upset that the Combined Werewolf and Vampire Trapping Expedition had come to an end—but I wasn't. Werewolves and vampires are not as easy to catch as you might think, and bedtime suddenly felt like a good idea.

We were just getting near the boiler room when Wanda suddenly stopped, and Uncle Drac and I nearly tripped over her. Wanda is a bit like one of those wind-up clockwork toys that suddenly run out of steam and stop when you least expect it. She is also not an awful lot bigger than a wind-up clockwork toy, so it is not surprising that she gets tripped over all the time. She should be used to it by now but she always makes a huge fuss—except this time she didn't.

"Give me the net!" she hissed at me. *"Quick!"*

I gave her the net. When Wanda hisses at you like that you do what she asks. She has a very bossy hiss. I didn't see what happened next because my stupid hologram glasses—which I had totally forgotten I was wearing on the top of my head—slipped down over my eyes and all I could see were two dark blobs. By the time I had figured out what had happened and pushed the glasses out of the way the werewolf trapping net was full—of Vampire Max.

I was very impressed. Wanda looked as if she had been netting vampires all her life. She lay on the floor holding on to the handle of the net as though her life depended on it, and there was no chance that Vampire Max could make a run for it. The net fitted him just right. It covered him from head to toe and he just stood there with his little arms at his sides like he knew the game was up. It is hard to see someone's expression when they are underneath a Combined Werewolf and Vampire Trapping Net, but Vampire Max did not look happy—and neither did Uncle Drac.

Uncle Drac knelt down beside Vampire Max and peered at him. He looked worried. "Be careful, Wanda," Uncle Drac said. "This could be dangerous." I was glad that Uncle Drac knew that Max was dangerous. At least we did not have to persuade *him* that Vampire Max had to go home. Then, very carefully, as though he was afraid Vampire Max would bite, Uncle Drac lifted off the net. Vampire Max did not move. He just stood there, totally covered in cobwebs and spiders, staring into space with empty eyes.

But there was something much worse than his weird vampire eyes: Vampire Max had blood dripping off his long pointy teeth.

Who had he bitten?

~13~

VAMPIRE CAT

It did not take me long to realise that there was only one person Vampire Max could have bitten—Aunt Tabby. Brenda and Barry were always safely locked in their bedroom by ten o'clock, but Aunt Tabby had been watching vampire films in the furry bathroom when we started the Combined Werewolf and Vampire Trapping Expedition. *And* she had the door open.

"Uncle Drac, Uncle Drac!" I said. "We've got to find Aunt Tabby before it is too late."

"Shh," said Uncle Drac, who was still kneeling beside Vampire Max. He looked up and said, "I don't think finding Tabby would be a very good idea, Minty," he said. "Now you must both be quiet and we will take Max back to bed. It's dangerous to wake people up when they are sleepwalking."

"Sleepwalking?" I gasped. "He's not sleep-walking. He's *vampiring*."

"Shh!" said Uncle Drac again, rather sharply. I was shocked. Uncle Drac even looked annoyed and he *never* looks annoyed.

But Aunt Tabby was in danger and I had to get him to understand, so I said, "Max is a real *vampire*, Uncle Drac. He bites people. Look at his teeth. Look at the *blood*. *He has bitten Aunt Tabby*."

"Shh, Minty," whispered Uncle Drac. "You mustn't believe all those old stories. No one bites people any more. Not even my mother, ha ha."

"But he's got really sharp *biting* teeth, Uncle Drac. Like little needles."

"And so did I at his age, Minty. That's how they come through. They'll soon get blunt. Now we must get Max back to bed without waking him."

Usually I believe what Uncle Drac tells me, but not this time. He was just making excuses. What about the blood dripping from Max's mouth—how did he explain *that*?

Uncle Drac picked up Max and carried him along the basement corridor like he was a sleeping baby rather than a horrible little vampire brat. Wanda and I trailed after him, up the basement stairs, and as we trooped past the clock in the hall I saw Uncle Drac glance at it with a worried look. It was nearly one o'clock. He speeded up and Wanda and I had to run to keep up with him.

As we got close to the furry bathroom I could see the flickering light of the film streaking across the passageway out of the half-open door. But Uncle Drac did not care about Aunt Tabby one bit. He stormed right past the furry bathroom and did not even look inside—in fact I am sure he speeded up.

"Come on, Wanda," I said, pulling her towards the half-open door. "We have to go and rescue Aunt Tabby."

Wanda did not seem keen. "Do we have to?" she whispered.

"Yes," I told her. "Now come on—quick!" But Wanda would not budge. She hung on tight to the doorknob. Finally, I managed to pull her into the room.

It was weird in there. The vampire film was still playing, but because of the headphones there was no sound, just the whirr of the projector. The film was getting to the really exciting part. The vampire, who looked very elegant and handsome, was creeping along the roof of a snow-covered castle in the middle of a forest. You could tell he was heading for the window that the heroine was desperately trying to close. You just *knew* that she would not be able to. In fact you wondered why she bothered to try in the first place, but heroines always do.

I could see the back of Aunt Tabby's head

and the weird shape of the headphones over her ears. The half-finished box of mint creams was on the floor beside her feet and it looked like nothing had happened at all. But that is how it is with vampires. They act so fast that you do not see them coming. And of course Vampire Max was really small—so Aunt Tabby wouldn't have seen him coming anyway, even if he hadn't been a vampire.

Suddenly I felt just like Wanda—I didn't want to rescue Aunt Tabby either. I was really scared of what I might find. But someone had to rescue her, and since there was no one else to do it, it would have to be me. I took a deep breath; then I marched over to the sofa and made myself look at Aunt Tabby. She was staring ahead at the movie screen with vacant eyes—like people always do when they have been bitten—so although I couldn't see any blood, I knew that Vampire Max had done his worst.

"Aunt Tabby!" I yelled, shaking her really hard. "Oh, Aunt Tabby, wake up, *wake up!*"

Aunt Tabby jumped like she had had an electric shock. She leaped to her feet, threw off her headphones, and screamed, "*Aaaaaaaaaaaargh!*" My ears went funny. Aunt Tabby stared down at me as though she was trying to work out what was happening, and then she yelled really, really fast so that all the words sounded stuck together: "OhmygoodnessAramintawhatare-you*doing*? You nearly gave me a heart attack! Why aren't you in bed?"

It was then the clock downstairs struck thirteen and Aunt Tabby looked at her watch. "It's one o'clock in the morning," she gasped. "What are you doing up so late? And where is Drac?"

Aunt Tabby obviously did not realise what a lucky escape she had had. Uncle Drac came rushing in.

"Tabby," he said, really worried—*at last*. "Tabby, what's the matter? Are you all right?"

"Only just, Drac," said Aunt Tabby, her voice sounding a bit trembly. "Araminta crept up on me and gave me the fright of my life. I really don't know what has got into her." She sat down on the old sofa and began fanning herself with the top of the box of mint creams.

"Oh, Minty," sighed Uncle Drac, "what *are* we going to do with you?" He smiled a tired-looking smile, gave me a big hug, and said to Aunt Tabby. "Minty has got it into her head that young Max is a vampire."

"What?" gasped Aunt Tabby.

"He's been eating those cherry sweets again."

"But I promised your mother I wouldn't let him *near* red sweets," groaned Aunt Tabby.

"Well, he obviously has a secret stash somewhere," said Uncle Drac.

Aunt Tabby gave a sigh. "So I suppose he's been sleepwalking?" she asked.

Uncle Drac nodded. "Don't worry, Tabby. He's fine. He didn't wake up. And now he's fast asleep in the Tuesday bedroom. Couldn't face that rope ladder contraption."

Huh, I thought. So Vampire Max has got the Tuesday bedroom now as well. Before long we'll be spending the whole week in the Friday bedroom—if he doesn't get that as well.

The reel of film suddenly came to an end and started whizzing round the projector.

Uncle Drac leaped up to rescue it.

Aunt Tabby fixed Wanda and me with a classic Aunt Tabby look and said, "Bed!"

We scooted off to the attic.

We tiptoed past the Tuesday bedroom and by the door was a scrunched-up paper bag. I picked it up because Aunt Tabby says, "If you see litter, don't just leave it lying there, Araminta. Pick it up and *put it in the bin*." I picked it up, but I did not put it in the bin. Certainly not. There was something in the bag and I knew what it was.

"Look, Wanda, here're Max's cherry sweets. Do you want one?" I knew she would take one because Wanda never says no to sweets. She rooted around in the bag like she always does to find the biggest one and put it in her mouth.

"Arn chew havin un?" Wanda said with her mouth full.

I shook my head. No way was I going to touch a bag of sweets that Vampire Max had had his sticky paws in all day. Anyway, this was an experiment, and a true scientist does not take part in her experiments. She observes the results. And that is what I did. The results were amazing.

Dribbles of red cherry juice ran down Wanda's chin as she chewed. And the more she chewed, the more the juice ran down. It was amazing. It looked just like blood. Wanda Wizzard was a vampire!

The next morning Aunt Tabby told us that Max was going home on Saturday and we had to be nice to him until then, and if we heard him sleepwalking again we must come and tell her right away. I reckoned we could manage that, seeing as he was going soon.

Once we let Max join in with things, he stopped being so creepy with Aunt Tabby and Brenda. Later that morning we met Sir Horace taking Fang for a walk around Spook House. Sir Horace—who does not usually walk much at all—wanted a rest, so he let us take Fang instead. It was great. Having a ghost wolf to take for a walk is the best thing ever. We showed Fang—and Max—all over Spook House and they saw all the really interesting places. The only place Fang would not go was Creepy Corner, past the bat poo hatch. The hair went up on his back and he growled a really horrible growl.

Suddenly there was a loud screech. Two

green werewolf eyes appeared out of no-where—and the next thing we knew a great big Pusskins-sized ball of fluff landed right in the middle of Fang. Fang howled and Pusskins spat and stuck out her claws.

"Pusskins!" yelled Wanda. She tried to pick her up, but Pusskins ran off into Creepy Corner.

That was where we found the kittens. Three tiny black kittens curled up on top of Uncle Drac's pile of bat poo sacks. Wanda thought they were even cuter than Fang, but I preferred Fang myself.

Brenda was thrilled. When Wanda told her, she did a Pusskins-style screech all her own. Brenda brought Pusskins and her kittens into the boiler room where it was warm, but Pusskins took her kittens straight back to

Creepy Corner. Then Brenda brought them back to the boiler room again and Pusskins took them back. Pusskins won in the end and Brenda ended up sitting in Creepy Corner too.

I was still not happy going to Creepy Corner. I had realised that the green were-wolf eyes were Pusskins' and they were up high because she was sitting on top of the pile of sacks. But I hadn't figured out the foot-prints—those were far too big for Pusskins. Did that mean there was a werewolf still lurk-ing in Spook House?

Just in case there was, I still wore my back-pack with the Combined Werewolf and Vampire Trapping Kit—even though we didn't need the vampire part any more.

On Saturday Wanda and I helped Max pack his coffin. We all carried it downstairs and waited for the hearse to arrive. Then Max said he wanted to say goodbye to the kittens. When we got there, Barry was shovelling bat poo and Brenda was feeding Pusskins some milk and fish. Pusskins looked a lot thinner now that she had had her kittens, but I could see that would not last long if Brenda kept bringing her food all the time.

Max said goodbye to the kittens. He looked quite sad, I thought. Then he said goodbye to Brenda without being creepy at all. He just said, "Goodbye, Brenda," and kept stroking his favourite kitten, a little black one with two white spots on either side of its mouth, just like vampire teeth.

Brenda said, "Goodbye, Max. Thank you for helping with the boiler. Perhaps you would like a kitten when they are big enough to leave Pusskins?"

Max smiled a huge, vampire smile and his pointy teeth flashed. But I didn't worry now, as I knew Uncle Drac was telling the truth; that when Max was older they would not be pointy anymore, but friendly, just like Uncle Drac's teeth.

"Yes, *please*," said Max. "I'd like this one."

"Then the little vampire cat is yours," said Brenda.

Max was so excited he ran straight through the bat poo and scooted along the corridor. It was then I noticed the werewolf footprints—

they were coming from Max's shoes! I nudged Wanda. "Look," I said, "it's Max making those werewolf footprints."

"I know," said Wanda.

"You know? *How?*"

"I thought *you* were the detective," said Miss Smug Pants.

"I can't be a detective and a vampire and werewolf hunter all at the same time," I told her. "Sometimes you have to delegate."

"You have to what?" asked Wanda.

"Delegate. Get someone else to do it. Like how I have *you* to find out about the werewolf prints—see?"

"Oh. Well, I noticed when he was kneeling down doing his packing. He's got a big wolf paw print thingy on the bottom of each shoe, so that when he runs he makes wolf prints instead of footprints. Isn't that fun? I'd like some fairy footprint shoes."

"Fairies don't make footprints," I told her. "They fly."

Before Wanda had a chance to answer there was a loud knock on the door and we raced to get it. I got there first, even before Aunt Tabby.

Standing on the doorstep was the almost grown-up girl. On her own!

"Hello, Mathilda," I said in my best grown-up voice. "Would you like to come in?"

"Yes, please, Araminta," she said. I was amazed. She remembered my name!

Then she said, like I was almost grown-up too, "I do hope Max has not been too much trouble."

So I smiled and said, "Not at all. We're

sorry to see him go." Which we were. And then I said, "I'll go and ask Barry to help Perkins with the trunk. Would you like a cup of tea before you go?"

And Mathilda smiled and said, "That would be wonderful, Araminta. Thank you."

So I took her downstairs to the third-kitchen-on-the-right-just-around-the-corner-past-the-boiler-room and I made the tea.

Aunt Tabby didn't say anything. She looked like she had just swallowed a tennis ball and was trying to work out what to do next. In fact she didn't say anything at all until we had waved goodbye to Max and Mathilda and the hearse had disappeared round the last bend. Then she said, "Well, Araminta, I must say you have picked up some wonderful manners from little Maximilian."

I didn't say anything because Aunt Tabby would not understand.

"Come on, Wanda," I said, "let's go and see if Max has left any sweets behind."

And we sat in our Saturday bedroom and ate three banana chews, five rhubarb and

custards, ten pink shrimps, four toffees, one piece of fudge, two strawberry chews, and a whole bar of fruit and nut chocolate.

When I grow up I want to be just like Mathilda. But not yet.

ANGIE SAGE, the celebrated author of the Septimus Heap series, shares her house with three ghosts who are quite shy. Two of the ghosts walk up and down the hall every now and then, while the other one sits and looks at the view out of the window. All three are just about the nicest ghosts you would ever wish to meet. She lives in England.

JIMMY PICKERING studied animation and has worked for Hallmark, Disney, and Universal Studios. He is the illustrator of several picture books.

VISIT ARAMINTA ONLINE!

Go to www.aramintaspook.co.uk to play games, download spooky colouring sheets, and learn more about the inhabitants of Spook House.